Angels

The BBC television series

Cast

1st year student Patricia Rutherford	Fiona Fullerton
1st year student Maureen Morahan	Erin Geraghty
2nd year student Jo Longhurst	Julie Dawn Cole
3rd year student Sita Patel	Karan David
3rd year student Shirley Brent	Clare Clifford
3rd year student Ruth Fullman	Lesley Dunlop
Senior Tutor Heather Windrup	Faith Brook
Sister Easby	June Watson

Writers

Adele Rose, Jill Hyem, Deborah Mortimer, Anne Valery, Len Rush, Pat Hooker, P. J. Hammond, Alan Janes, Leslie Duxbury

Directors

Julia Smith, Derek Martinus, Ken Hannam, Valerie Hanson, Michael Briant, John Gorrie, Ron Craddock

Hospital Complex designed by Barrie Dobbins
Developed and edited by Paula Milne
Produced by Ron Craddock

Paula Milne, after graduating from the Central School of Art and Design, spent three years studying film-making at the Royal College of Art. From there she went on to write scripts for the ATV serial *Crossroads* and in 1973 joined the BBC. The characters for the BBC series *Angels* were created by her and she is also Script Editor for the series. She is twenty-seven years old.

Leslie Duxbury was a journalist on the *News Chronicle* and *Daily Express* before he went freelance some twenty years ago, helped to run a news agency and began writing for television in his spare time. This is now his main occupation and his work includes scripts for *Coronation Street*, *Z-Cars*, *Her Majesty's Pleasure* (his own comedy series) and *Hunter's Walk*. He keeps in journalistic trim by writing soccer reports for the *Observer*.

Paula Milne
and Leslie Duxbury

Angels

A Pan original
Pan Books and the British Broadcasting Corporation

First published 1975 by Pan Books Ltd,
Cavaye Place, London SW10 9PG,
and the British Broadcasting Corporation,
35 Marylebone High Street, London W1M 4AA
2nd printing 1976

ISBN 0 330 24661 5 (Pan)
ISBN 0 563 17001 8 (BBC)
Made and printed in Great Britain by
Hazell Watson & Viney Ltd, Aylesbury, Bucks

Foreword

ANGELS – not the heavenly kind, but Nurses. These 'Angels' have their feet on the ground in St Angela's Hospital, Battersea: that is how the name 'Angels' was derived.

St Angela's Hospital itself was named after the saint who was born in Desenzano on Lake Garda in Northern Italy in 1474. St Angela was a devout girl who devoted most of her life to teaching children. Her work became known, and a group of nuns joined her under the patronage of St Ursula. Angela Merici is now known as the founder of the Ursuline Nuns.

St Angela's Hospital, Battersea has an affinity with Angela Merici in that it is both a teaching institution and a caring establishment. It was built in the first decade of the twentieth century, part of the growth of hospital building that occurred in the post-Nightingale era. Since it was built, however, there have been many additions – connecting corridors between the blocks (patients used to be wheeled from one block to the other through the rain or snow), nurses' home, outpatients' annexe, emergency area, and maternity, psychiatric and geriatric units. Within, many structural alterations have been made to accommodate some of the equipment which has developed as a result of modern hospital technology.

The hospital has twenty-four wards of assorted sizes housing over seven hundred beds. It overlooks Battersea Park and the old Festival Gardens. Battersea Power Station can be seen nearby from the top floors of the hospital. Not far away is Clapham Junction and the new Covent Garden Market at Vauxhall. Across the visually interesting Albert Bridge over the Thames lies Chelsea. Senior nursing staff and those nurses – like Jo, Ruth and Shirley – who are not accommodated in the nurses' home, live in these areas.

These three girls, together with Sita, Maureen and Patricia, are what the following pages are all about – young women, between eighteen and twenty-one years old, learning their profession as nurses: a career which, despite its inevitable involvement with distress, care and pain, does sometimes have its lighter moments.

RON CRADDOCK
Producer 'Angels'

St. Angela's Hospital

MERICI ROAD
LONDON S.W. 11

HOSPITAL SCHOOL OF NURSING
CONFIDENTIAL REPORT

Surname Brent **Forenames** Shirley Susan

Date of birth 23/7/53 **Expected date of final examination** Autumn 1975

Previous nursing or other relevant qualifications None

Confidential report

During her three-year training, Shirley has shown herself to be a scrupulously careful, conscientious nurse. Her ward reports have been unfailingly complimentary about her diligent attitude, but sometimes ward sisters have shown concern about Shirley's inability to use her initiative. She has a tendency to do things by the book, instead of using her own discretion. Shirley lives alone, and is something of a 'loner'. She is a rather selfconscious, even shy girl who finds it difficult to make friends. This makes her over-conscientious and constantly on her guard at work, as though she were terrified of failure. Perhaps once she passes her SRN exam she will gain confidence and be able to relax more.

Heather Windrup

Heather Windrup, Senior Nursing Tutor

SHIRLEY 'Mr Weaver,' I said firmly. 'Will you *please* get back into bed.'

'I will not.' He looked at me over his shoulder. 'Oh, it's you, Matron.'

He was leaning out of an open window in the side ward, staring at the street beyond: his head was still bandaged from his operation.

'See that,' he said, nodding towards the view. I crossed and stood next to him. Battersea Park stretched away in front of us, and beyond it I could just see the river, glinting in the sun.

'See what?' I asked.

'All of it.' He put his elbows on the sill and stared out. 'It's all going on out there.'

'You really shouldn't be standing by this open window, you know.'

'People going places . . . doing things. Like that feller there . . .' He pointed to a small, purposeful figure striding through the Park, hands in pockets, head down. 'Where d'you reckon he's off to?'

I stood on tiptoe to get a better view. 'Probably on his way home from work.'

'At three in the afternoon?' Weaver said disparagingly. 'No, he's off to an assignation. A secret meeting.'

'How d'you know?'

'It's obvious, isn't it?'

'Not to me it's not.'

'You've no imagination, my girl.'

Beneath us the man turned out of the Park and crossed the road out of sight.

'Why else would he be walking like that?' Weaver continued. 'Not looking around at anything or anyone?'

'And that adds up to a secret assignation, does it?'

'Well . . .' Weaver drearily turned away from the window, suddenly losing interest. 'I've got to pass the time somehow, haven't I? So I invent things for people. Kills a few minutes if nothing else.'

'Will you go back to bed now?' I asked.

'If you say so.' He climbed onto his bed, not under the sheets, but on top of them. He stretched out and put his hands on his head.

'You know what?' he said, his eyes on the ceiling.

'What?' I closed the window, abruptly cutting off the sounds of the street below.

'I don't reckon I'm ever going to get out of here.'

'Don't talk rubbish, Mr Weaver!'

'It's rubbish, is it?'

'You know very well it is.' I busied myself by picking up his chart at the end of the bed.

'Tell me something, Matron.' He looked at me, suddenly earnest. We were in a small side ward off Male Surgery and outside I could hear the Auxiliary serving tea, clattering the crockery and tonelessly singing a theme song from some television programme.

'Where d'you see yourself in a year's time?'

'A year's time?' I frowned. 'Well . . . I'll be qualified by then, I suppose.'

'And?'

'I could be anywhere.'

'But you can imagine yourself somewhere, though? Somewhere specific?'

'Yes . . .' I was puzzled by the question.

'I can't, you see.' He rolled his eyes back at the ceiling. 'I can't see myself doing anything in a year's time. I can't even picture it.'

'Well, you've been in hospital a long time, you've got a bit disorientated.'

'It's a funny feeling.' He spoke absentmindedly, his head still resting on his arms, his eyes looking at the ceiling. 'Like there's no future. Like me life has run in a line, a hard, straight line, and then gradually the line starts to peter out.' He paused and then added, 'Not with a bang, but a whimper.'

'Pardon?'

He abruptly smiled at me, showing a row of nicotine-stained teeth. 'It's a poem. By Eliot.' The smile faded and he said in a flat voice, 'This is the way the world ends, this is the way the world ends, not with a bang but a whimper.'

There was a rustle of starch at the door and Sister Easby entered.

'Ah, Nurse Brent.' She caught sight of Mr Weaver staring at the ceiling. 'And how are we feeling now, Mr Weaver?'

'We,' said Mr Weaver, carefully enunciating the word, 'are feeling bloody awful.'

'Doctor'll be round soon,' said Sister. 'He'll give you something.'

Weaver smiled faintly at her. 'Something for nothing.'

'I beg your pardon?'

He looked at her for a moment, then turned to me.

'Can you draw the blinds, Nurse? I think I'll get a bit of the old shut-eye.'

I moved to the window and started to lower the blind.

'Pop into my office when you've done, Nurse Brent,' said Sister, perfunctorily patting Weaver's bed as she went out.

I continued to pull the blind right down, plunging the room into sudden darkness. Weaver didn't stir and I cautiously made my way to the door. Then his voice suddenly came out of the gloom at me.

'Matron?'

I turned back. 'Yes?'

'It's called *The Hollow Men.*'

'What is?'

'That poem.'

'Oh.' I hesitated, uncertain if he'd finished.

'You should read it some time.' He sounded drowsy and I turned to go again, but pulled up.

'Why d'you call me that?' I asked curiously.

'What?'

'Matron. You're always calling me Matron.'

He didn't answer and I opened the door, assuming he'd fallen asleep. Then he said: 'It suits you, that's why.'

Sister Easby always reminded me of a games teacher we had at school. She had the same cropped hair and athletic spring to her step. Easby is one of those people who live the clean life. She doesn't smoke, drinks sherry very occasionally and likes walking. Not for her the furred tongue of a hangover or the guilty joy of a late morning in bed.

She was on the telephone when I entered her office, talking to a Medical Social Worker. She absently waved me to a seat and carried on, the phone hooked over her shoulder while she busied herself sorting out a pile of X-rays on the desk.

I sat down and waited for her to finish. Through the window behind her I could see a small square of brilliant blue sky. It was good to sit down, and under the cover of her desk, I gently eased my foot out of my shoe and stretched my cramped toes. Sister replaced the phone and looked at me vaguely.

'Yes, Nurse Brent?'

'You said you wanted to see me, Sister.'

'Did I?' Her face cleared. 'Of course. Your Appraisal.* Have you time now?'

'Well . . .' I hesitated. I'd forgotten all about my Appraisal. 'There's Mr Knight's pre-med to see to . . .'

'I'll get one of the others on to it. You stay here.'

While she was out of the room I picked up a letter from her desk. It said: 'Dear Sister.' The writing was sloping and faint. 'I am writing to inquire about the condition of Mr Feather, my brother, who was admitted to your ward last weekend.' I slid the letter under the X-rays and leant back, trying to recollect who Mr Feather was. He must have been that timid little man in the bed by the Day Room, who was always terribly polite. Even at the end he was polite. Staff Nurse and I had stayed with him, and I remember he had said: 'I'm sorry to be so much trouble. Really I am.' And then he quietly went. I slid my foot back into my shoe and straightened myself in my seat as Sister came back into the room. She shut the door and smiled at me.

'Right, this shouldn't take long, Nurse.'

She crossed to her desk and sat down, shifting the letters and X-rays to one side. Opening her drawer she pulled out a Nurse Appraisal form and placed it on the blotter in front of her.

'I don't want this to be too formal, Nurse Brent,' she said briskly, unscrewing her pen cap. 'I've already filled in the form

*An Appraisal is a kind of frank interview given by the ward sister to a student nurse at the end of her eight-week stint on the ward. The form is then sent to the Nursing Tutor. In that way she can monitor the progress of her students outside the classroom.

and there's really nothing to add about your work except that you have the makings of a very efficient and capable nurse.'

'Thank you, Sister.'

'You're a very reliable member of the ward team,' she went on, flashing me a brief smile. 'And you don't avoid taking responsibility, which is important for a future staff nurse.'

I was about to thank her again when I remembered I already had, so I said nothing.

'The thing I want to discuss with you . . .' Sister hesitated, fiddling with the corner of the form. 'Is really of a more personal nature.'

'Oh?' I waited for her to go on.

'First of all . . . Have you any particular problems you'd like to talk to me about?'

'Problems, Sister?'

'Family trouble. Financial problems. Anything like that?'

'No, Sister.'

'Good.' She put her pen down and placed her hands flat on the table, staring at me. 'You live alone, don't you?'

'Yes, Sister. I've a bedsit.'

'Have you ever thought of sharing?'

'Sharing?' I asked, puzzled by the question.

'With a friend. Another nurse, perhaps.'

'Not really, no.'

'You like living on your own?'

I frowned, wondering where all this was leading. 'I've got used to it, I suppose.'

'I'm bringing this up, Nurse, because I think it's relevant to your attitude towards your co-workers and patients.'

She was watching me closely, waiting for me to react.

'I don't quite understand, Sister,' I said at last.

'It's a question of manner, Nurse,' she said. 'You often seem . . . unrelaxed and tense on the ward. I know you're a serious girl and nursing means a lot to you, but sometimes that seriousness can be misinterpreted.'

'Misinterpreted?'

'By the patients for instance.' She pulled open a drawer and took out a packet of mints, offering me one. I shook my head.

'You so rarely smile. Sometimes they need someone to smile and joke with them, particularly when they're feeling depressed and anxious about themselves.'

I thought of Mr Weaver, as he recited the line of that poem of his in the side ward.

'There's more to nursing than just ensuring the patient's physical wellbeing is catered for,' Sister went on in a routine voice. 'Their mental state must be considered as well. And that means a flexibility of attitude on the part of the nurse. If a patient is depressed, he might need gently coaxing out of it. Be made to relax more and forget about himself. I don't mean that you should be frivolous or hysterical, but just the occasional smile. The odd bit of small talk here and there.'

I looked down at my hands resting on my apron. 'I do try, Sister.'

'I know.' She sounded sympathetic and just a little awkward. 'It's a struggle if that kind of thing doesn't come naturally, but it is important that you persevere. You've a rather . . .' She paused, searching for the words. 'Stiff manner. A tendency to do everything by the book. But we're dealing with people, and you can't place them into neat little categories and procedures. You must try and relax a bit. Bend your own rules occasionally.'

'Yes, Sister.' I wasn't sure what she was getting at, but it was easier to accept her advice than question it.

'It applies to your workmates as well,' she continued in her lilting Scottish voice. 'You set yourself such high standards, Nurse, and expect others to adhere to those standards. If they don't . . .' She shrugged. 'You become intolerant and snap at them. You must try and accept the fact that you have weaknesses, and having done that, you might find yourself able to be more tolerant of weakness in others. Do you understand what I am getting at?'

'I think so, Sister,' I said, and then added resentfully, 'but if I am intolerant, it's because the job is so important to me.'

'I realize that.' She was smiling at me reassuringly. 'And it's very good that it is. But you're young. You can't live your whole life in this hospital. You should be getting out, enjoying yourself, making friends . . . The job won't suffer because of it. If anything it'll improve because you'll be happy and fulfilled outside it.'

I didn't speak for a moment, digesting her words. She was looking at me with that thin smile of hers, her head tilted slightly to one side.

'Who says I'm not happy and fulfilled outside it?' I asked sullenly.

'I do, Nurse.' The smile faded just a fraction. 'Why else do you stay late after every shift? Why else do you never talk about your social life, or boyfriends or parties like the other girls?'

'Just because I don't talk about it . . .'

'I understand your pride, Shirley.' The sudden use of my christian name made me start. 'And normally I wouldn't think of prying into a girl's private life, but in your case it's affecting your work. So let's try and put our feelings aside, shall we, and talk in practicalities?'

I noted the use of the royal 'we', the same term as she used on the ward when addressing a patient. 'And how are we feeling now, Mr Weaver?'

'This bedsitter.' Sister's voice was suddenly firm and authoritative. 'Is it in a private house or what?'

'It's a sort of boarding-house. There are three or four bedsits in it.'

'And how do you get on with the other people?'

I thought of the closed doors. The brief nods on the stairs to the other guests.

'I don't see much of them,' I said. 'My hours tend . . .'

'And what do you do when you're off-duty?' she interrupted. 'Do you go out or . . . ?'

'I study a lot. Go to the cinema sometimes.'

'With friends?'

'Of course,' I lied.

'I see.' She fell silent for a second, rolling her fountain pen around on her blotter. In the corridor outside, the tea trolley was being rattled into the lift, the ward-maids shouting instructions to each other.

'I'm going to make a suggestion, Nurse,' said Sister finally. 'I want you to seriously consider sharing a flat. Put a notice up in the recreation room. Look in the evening papers . . . I'm sure living by yourself is at the root of the problem. If you had to live with others you'd learn to relax more, accept other people's idiosyncrasies, and more importantly, have someone to chat things over with. Discuss your problems, so that you can see them in perspective. You're far too young to be taking life so seriously.'

She smiled dismissively. 'All right?'

'Yes, Sister.'

'Good girl.' The interview was clearly at an end, so I stood up.

'Don't forget to sign it.' She pushed the Appraisal form over to me, offering me her fountain pen with the other hand. Then I did a stupid thing. In a moment of petulant pride, I refused the offer of her pen, reaching for my own in my uniform pocket. Sister smiled faintly and replaced her pen in the drawer. I signed the form without really looking at it and gave it back. Sister took it and folded it in half, glancing at me as she did so.

'There's nothing to be ashamed of, you know,' she said.

'Ashamed?'

'It happens to the best of us.' She smiled ironically. 'Like Mr Weaver out there. Too proud to admit he's lonely. He refused to go into the main ward with the rest, so he mopes about on his own, and won't let any of us near enough to help him.'

It seemed an odd comparison, to compare Mr Weaver with me, and it took me a moment to comprehend what she meant. It had never struck me before that Weaver was lonely, any more than it had about myself. I remembered my conversation with him, and his simple conviction that he would never get out of hospital. Dutifully I recounted it to Sister, who listened and then said: 'Has he asked about the results of his tests yet?'

'No, Sister. He just seems to think . . .'

'That they'll be positive.' Sister frowned. 'He's taken a very pessimistic line about it all along.'

'Do you think he has cause?'

'We won't know until the biopsy result comes through. And even if it is positive, there's every chance that surgery might help.' She stood up and walked with me to the door. 'When you get the chance, have another go at him. See if he'll agree to going into the main ward. It's not going to do him any good lying there thinking the worst.'

I didn't manage to see Mr Weaver before I went off duty. He was asleep at four o'clock and I was too preoccupied with my interview with Sister to think about very much else. On the way home I bought an evening paper and after I'd made myself a meal I sat and studied the FLATS TO LET column. I still felt resentful about my Appraisal and Sister's suggestion, but at the same time I found it rather appealing. I had shared a flat when I first came to London, three years before, with a couple of other nurses. I had enjoyed it, but after a couple of months the lease was terminated and we had to move out. The other two had moved into a bedsitter in Earls Court and I had to come here. I glanced around at the faded wallpaper and limp candlewick bedspread. I had intended it to be temporary, but somehow the time had slipped by and I had never moved . . . My eyes roved down the list of flats in the paper. There were very few furnished flats advertised and most seemed exorbitantly expensive. Then my eye caught one right at the bottom . . .

5th gl. rqd. mxd. flat. SE11. Own rm. c.h. £8. pw. Phone Tony . . .

The flat turned out to be in Vauxhall. It took several attempts to get through on the phone, and when I did I was told viewing was from six onwards. Clutching my A–Z I wandered around the grimy backstreets of the neighbourhood until finally I found the road. It was a crumbling terraced street with a large mansion block dominating it at one end. The mansion block proved to be the address I was looking for, and after climbing several flights of steps, I found myself outside flat No 22.

There was already a queue of girls waiting, most of whom had obviously been there for some time. Some were seated on the bare, tiled floor, others were sprawled over the steps. I counted nine girls in all and was just contemplating whether it was worth staying when the door opened and a tall, bespectacled young man in a denim suit ushered out a couple of girls and then signalled for two more to go in. He glanced vaguely over the rest of us who were still waiting, did a rapid head count, and then retreated back into the flat. It was a good ten minutes before the door opened again and the next two went in. I shuffled further up the queue and looked at the girls still waiting. Some looked very young, hardly more than seventeen, with heavily blacked-up eyes and an aggressive sort of confidence. We all eyed each other suspiciously until finally it was my turn to go in.

The denim-suited young man turned out to be Tony, and after he'd got us inside and shut the door, he efficiently produced a notebook and started taking down details. There was another girl with me who had been in front of me in the queue, and he asked her name, present address, phone number and occupation. She was a telephonist with a nervous giggle. She told him she was nineteen, lived at home but wanted a place of her own because her parents disapproved of her boyfriend who was black. At the mention of her boyfriend Tony wrote something down in the notebook next to her name and turned to me.

'And you are?'

'Shirley Brent.'

He wrote it down and then asked for my address. When he'd noted that, he asked my occupation.

'I'm a nurse.'

'A nurse?' He glanced at me sharply through the thick lenses of his glasses. 'Where d'you nurse?'

'St Angela's. Battersea.'

'Ah, yes.'

Another young man sidled down the corridor towards us. He was shorter than Tony, with a shock of angry red hair. When Tony told him I was a nurse, he too turned to look at me.

'A nurse, eh?'

'That's right.'

He and Tony exchanged a glance and the tour around the flat began. There were five bedrooms in all, the one going for let being the smallest. I liked it immediately. It was long and narrow, with one wall painted a faded yellowish colour, which gave the whole room a sort of warm glow. At the far end was a large bay window, which stretched from the floor to the ceiling, and just in front of the window, a low double bed with an old Indian quilt on it. I didn't have time to get more than a brief impression of the room before we were hustled off to see the bathroom and kitchen. The kitchen was large and utilitarian, with a big wooden table in the middle of it.

Another young man stood at the stove, stirring something in a large cauldron. He was shabbily dressed like the others, with straggly brown hair and tinted glasses. He was introduced as Paul and he nodded briefly before continuing with his stirring. I crossed to him and looked into the saucepan. He was boiling up some garment which gave off a sickly, sweet smell.

'It's a T-shirt,' he said by way of explanation. 'I'm dyeing it brown.'

'Oh.'

An awkward pause followed, and I tried to think of something to say, but Paul got there first.

'What d'you reckon on the room?'

'I like it.'

'It's a bit on the small side.'

There was a piece of paper sellotaped to the wall behind him and I leaned over to look at it.

'It's a duty rota,' he said.

'Oh?'

He lifted up the wooden spoon he'd been using to stir his dye and pointed to the names.

'Monday's Tony.' He broke off. 'You've met Tony, haven't you?'

'Yes.'

'Well, Mondays Tony has to cook. Tuesdays Bill does it.' He gestured vaguely towards the redheaded bloke who was earnestly explaining the merits of an old refrigerator to another prospective tenant.

'Wednesday's Val's turn, God help us.'

'Val?'

'You haven't met her. She's a lousy cook. And Thursday's me. And that blank space . . .' He pointed to a space under Friday. 'Is for whoever moves in.'

'I see. So there are . . . ?'

'Four of us in all.' He grinned at me. 'Five counting the new tenant.'

At that moment Tony appeared and interrupted us.

'Sally's a nurse,' he told Paul in a pointed kind of way.

'Shirley,' I said.

He stared at me vacantly.

'My name's Shirley,' I said again.

'I thought it was Sally.' The thick lenses of his glasses gave him a shifty, almost furtive look.

'Nurses are top of our list,' he announced in a rather grand tone.

'Oh?'

'He means our priority list,' said Paul quickly.

'We always put hardship cases first,' Tony added.

'I don't know that I'm a hardship case exactly,' I replied defensively. 'I can afford the rent if that's what you mean.'

'But you're not exactly rolling in it, are you?' Tony pointed out in his pompous tone. 'Anyway, I haven't shown you the sitting-room yet. This way.'

They promised they'd ring me, but three days later I'd still heard nothing. When they finally did ring, I was on duty. Mr Weaver was still in his side ward and I was making another attempt to persuade him to go into the main ward. It was just after lunch and his plate of uneaten food lay on the trolley over the bed. He was propped up against a bank of pillows, his arms lying limply over the sheets. He looked like a dummy we used in the training school, with his bandaged, shaved head, and his pallid face.

'Let me get this straight, Nurse,' he said in a dreary voice. 'You want me to go into the main ward, not because someone might be needing this bed, but because you think it would be better for me?'

'That's right.'

'Better for me physically or mentally?' he asked.

'Well . . . both.'

'I see.' He shut his eyes. 'Don't you think I'm the best judge of that?'

'Sister thought . . . You're not going to help yourself by staying in here alone worrying about yourself, are you?'

He slowly opened his eyes and looked at me expressionlessly.

'Of course, if you want me to go into there,' he said, 'I'm

powerless to stop you. But let me assure you of one fact, Matron. I enjoy being by myself. I prefer it. Besides . . .' He paused, and one hand fluttered up to his eyes. 'I've certain preparations to make.'

'Preparations?'

'Yes, preparations. You know what I mean.' He moved around restlessly in the bed.

'I don't know why you talk like this,' I said. 'We haven't had the results of your biopsy yet . . .'

'I don't need the results. I know them already.'

I stared at him.

'I'm not a fool, Nurse,' he went on in a flat tone. 'I can put two and two together. Death's not going to snatch me away unawares. No way.' He gave a short, cynical laugh. 'I'm going to be ready for her. Ready and waiting.' He was looking fixedly at me, defying me to challenge his words.

The moment was abruptly broken by Ruth Fullman putting her head round the door.

'Telephone call for you, Nurse.'

'For me?' I said, dragging my eyes off Weaver.

'In Sister's office.' She smiled at Mr Weaver. 'Not eating again, Mr Weaver? You're going to disappear one of these days.'

He smiled faintly back at her. 'You might be right at that.'

She grinned at him and went. Weaver turned to me, the limp smile still on his face.

'Must be the boyfriend.'

'It's probably about a flat I was after,' I told him. 'I've been expecting them to ring.'

'New horizons, eh?'

'Something like that.' I moved to the door. 'I'll tell Sister you'd rather stay here, then. But she might decide to transfer you anyway.'

'You tell her I'm too old.'

'Too old?'

'For new horizons.'

It was Tony on the phone. I recognized his sardonic voice immediately.

'You've the green light.' His voice was a distant crackle on the line.

'Pardon?'

'You're in, girl. The room's yours. Two weeks in advance and twenty-five quid deposit. Can you manage it?'

I did a rapid calculation in my head. 'Just about.'

'Good. Move in whenever you like. I'll give you the keys and so on when you arrive.'

I took a deep, exhilarated breath and started to thank him, but he'd already hung up. Sister, at her desk, was watching quizzically.

'I know you won't make a habit of accepting phone calls on the ward, Nurse,' she said pointedly. 'Not bad news, I hope?'

I absently straightened my apron, thinking about the yellow room and the blank space under the duty rota in the kitchen which would now have *my* name pencilled in under Friday. 'It was my flatmate,' I said with dignity, and after flashing her a quick, triumphant smile, I left the room.

Two days later I moved in. My old landlady, Mrs Levy, was obviously surprised at my sudden departure and told me I had been the perfect tenant. Despite my perfection, though, I had a hard job getting my deposit back off her, but after a long and earnest conversation in her draughty hall, she finally succumbed and gave it to me.

The girl Val was the only person in when I arrived with my taxi full of possessions. She was tall, dark and snubnosed and spoke with a blunt Northern accent. She introduced herself in an abrupt sort of way, looking me over curiously. Rather reluctantly she helped me in with my things and then left me to it. The room was just as I had remembered it, the yellow wall casting a warm light over everything, making even the threadbare carpet seem palatable.

I soon had my books up and my own things around me, and I sat on the bed for a while, savouring my new surroundings. I could hear sounds outside and I realized I ought to go out and make myself known. I did my hair and put on some eye makeup, and, feeling rather nervous, stepped out into the corridor.

There was a harsh jangle of pop music coming from the kitchen, and I went in to discover Val ironing. A transistor radio perched on a shelf behind her.

'Hello,' I said, rather selfconsciously. 'You look busy.'

'I start a new job tomorrow. Worse luck.' She grimaced, making her sour little face look suddenly old.

'What sort of job is that?'

'I'm a temp.' She held up the silk shirt she was ironing and scrutinized it. 'I thought I'd better turn up in something smart or else I'll get the chop again.'

There didn't seem much to say to that, so I put the kettle on. Val watched me curiously from the other end of the room.

'You're a nurse, I hear.'

'That's right.'

'Don't know how you can stand it. All those people dying and things.'

'You get used to it,' I replied rather inanely. 'Where are the cups kept?'

'Try the cupboard.' She paused for a moment, watching me, then asked curiously, 'Have you ever seen anyone die?'

'Oh yes.' I looked in the cupboard and a stale loaf of bread stared vacantly back at me.

'Actually die? In front of your eyes?'

'Several times.' I found a chipped mug and poured some milk into it.

'What's it like?'

'Well . . . like someone going to sleep, I suppose.'

'Oh.' She sounded vaguely disappointed.

The kitchen was cold and I stood in front of the cooker, warming my hands against the gas heating the kettle. Somewhere a door banged and Val said: 'That's probably Paul. He said he'd be home early.'

Footsteps sounded in the corridor and he came in. He looked startled to see me at first. Then he smiled.

'So, you've arrived.'

'About half an hour ago.' I felt oddly nervous as I turned to face him.

'Welcome to the madhouse.'

'Would you like a cup of tea?' I asked. 'I was just making some.'

'I'll do it. You sit down.' He moved to the cooker. 'Just come off duty have you?'

'I got today off.' I sat down and started playing with the sugar spoon, making even little rivulets in the glossy grains of sugar. Paul busied himself making tea. He was a precise sort of person and it showed in the way he carefully warmed the pot and then measured the tea into it. Val finished her ironing and then left the room. Paul poured out the tea and sat opposite me. Daylight was fading but we didn't switch the light on. Paul's glasses cast hollows round his eyes and threw forlorn shadows down his cheeks.

'You think you'll like it here?'

'I hope so,' I said. And I found myself telling him about the bedsitter and the fact that I had lived alone for the past three years.

'I admire people who can do that. Live alone. I know I couldn't.'

'There's nothing admirable about it,' I replied. 'I hadn't much choice.'

'Couldn't you share with one of your nursing friends?'

I hesitated a moment: he was watching me intently, and I could feel his breath on my face.

'I could have, I suppose,' I said finally. 'But to tell you the truth I don't seem to get on that well with other nurses.'

'Why's that?'

'I'm not sure.' I took a sip of tea and then said, 'It's my fault really.'

'Oh?'

I wondered why he was so interested. It was a long time since anyone had shown such an interest in me and I felt myself bristling with suspicion. As if it were some kind of card game we were playing, and he wanted me to expose my hand.

'The job's very important to me, you see,' I said carefully. 'I want to do well in it. To lots of the others . . . well, it's just a job. They might just as well be working in a factory or doing a catering course.'

'And you resent them?'

'No . . . well, yes, I suppose I do in a way. You see . . .'

He was still looking at me. The interest seemed genuine, yet it was hard to tell. I wished the light was on, so that I could see him more clearly.

'I never did very well at school,' I said with a rush. 'I was a real dumb-bell.' He was grinning and I went on quickly, 'No, really. I wasn't actually bottom of the class, but pretty near. If I had been bottom it would have been better. There's a certain status in being bottom of the class. Nothing's expected of you, you become the classroom clown. The mascot.'

'So what were you if you weren't bottom?'

'Seventeenth out of a class of twenty,' I replied, feeling my guard slowly being lowered. The darkened room and his gently probing questions were winning. I could feel the urge to confide in him growing as we talked.

'Not bottom, not top,' I went on. 'Not even halfway up. It was the never-never land of the sub-standard teens. I once made it to fourteenth,' I added with a wry smile. 'But it didn't last.'

He smiled and said, 'So you're going to succeed in nursing where you failed at school?'

'That's the idea, I suppose. I've never rationalized it before.'

'It's the old story,' he said. 'Of trying to prove yourself.'

'It's not just that. It's the patients too . . . The feeling that I'm of use. That I can help people.'

A light was suddenly snapped on in the hall and its brilliant beam shone into the room, throwing harsh linear shadows across Paul's cheeks. He lit a cigarette and started to tell me about the architectural course he was on, about his doubts and aspirations. As he talked I thought: this is what it is all about. What I've been missing all this time. Not just the exchanging of confidences, but the sense of discovering one's own beliefs through having to communicate them to others. I felt a sudden urge of exhilaration as I realized that this conversation could be the first of many.

It had never occurred to me before that proximity had anything to do with friendship. I had always believed that friendship depended on a scrupulously careful selection based on preconceived ideas about background and common interests. But sitting in that darkened room, I realized that it was a far more arbitrary affair. The simple fact of two people being flung together in close proximity was enough basis for a relationship; like neighbours within a street. They may not actively like each other, but they evolve a kind of intimacy between them that renders the selection of friends by background and common interest redundant. On the face of it, Paul and I had little in common. He was working-class, whilst I was definitely middle. His outlook was obviously more liberal than mine, and yet it didn't seem to matter. We had the shared experience of our daily environment. Of the mugs we drank from and taps dripping in the sink. And, or so it seemed to me on that first evening in my new home, this was ample basis upon which to build a relationship . . .

Sister was right, things did improve at work. Not all at once, but during a period of about a week. My off-duty hours ceased to be a listless void; I no longer found myself in the library killing time before going home; or acting the uneasy eavesdropper in canteen conversations. Recollecting these events, I wonder at how slow I was to catch on. The reason for my newly discovered elation was as obvious as it was trite. Paul. It is a humbling experience to realize that one person can have such an effect upon another. Of course it didn't seem humbling at the time. It seemed thrilling, like an adventure. I was like a ship setting out on an uncharted course.

My romantic entanglements, until that time, had numbered three. Firstly, an obsession with a teacher at school, then that was transferred to a boy at my old hospital (a medical student called Dave whom I had kissed fleetingly at a sweaty Christmas dance) and finally, about a year before, with a boy who briefly moved into the bedsitter above mine, but who subsequently moved away. And now there was Paul. I could see his window as I walked up the street towards the flat. If his light was on it meant sudden elation. A quickening of pace and an impatient rattling at the lift button. If the light was out, it meant a sluggish walk home and a dreary drag up the four flights to the front door. Followed by an internal bleakness that was only alleviated by the sound of his key in the door. But my inexperience afforded me enormous pleasure during those few days. Who else but the totally naive could receive such pleasure from a brief smile or a cursory nod? Such actions seemed to me to have imponderable importance, if only because they meant my presence was registered. I was content with even that, because I had only the vaguest idea of what could follow.

A few days after I moved in Tony suggested that they gave a party to welcome me. He sprang it quite suddenly after a meal one night. We had consumed an indigestibly salty spaghetti bolognaise cooked by Val, and were all seated around the dining-room table, too bloated to move. I was sitting on an orange box with a cushion perched on top because we were short of chairs. Paul was sitting next to me while Tony presided over us at the end of the table. Bill and Val had just started to clear the table when Tony suddenly brought the subject up.

'D'you like parties?' he asked unexpectedly, peering at me through his thick lenses.

'What sort of parties?' I asked rather stupidly.

'The bring your own bottle and plastic cup sort. The french bread and mousetrap cheese sort.'

'Why d'you ask?'

'Because we're thinking of giving one.'

I glanced at Paul, who looked oddly uneasy.

'By way of welcoming you to the flat,' Tony continued. 'Any excuse to have a party, I say.'

'There's really no need . . .'

'There's every need.' Tony's voice adopted its pompous tone. 'You meet our friends, we meet yours. That way we all get to know each other. See what I mean?'

'Well . . .'

'We all chip in, say a fiver, and make sure everyone brings some plonk with them, and Bob's your proverbial uncle. What about Saturday?'

'Saturday?'

'It's a bit short notice,' Paul said, shooting me a quick look. 'Maybe you'd like a bit more warning?'

'Oh no. Saturday should be fine. I'm on first shift that day.'

'Splendid.' Tony took out a cigarette packet and started to write on it. 'Now. We generally reckon on about ten people each which makes forty. What about you?'

'Me?'

'Guests.' He sounded wearily patient. 'Since it's in your honour I think you should have anything up to twenty.'

'Twenty!'

'The most important thing is to match people,' Tony went on. 'Now most of our friends . . .' – he indicated himself and Paul – 'are blokes from college and presumably most of yours are other nurses?' He looked at me quizzically. I felt obliged to respond in some way so I nodded.

'Excellent. Shouldn't have any problems at all then. Provided they don't all turn up with a feller in tow.'

By lunchtime next day I had succeeded in getting six girls to agree to come to the party. I popped into the canteen for a quick lunch before starting on duty and scoured the tables for a familiar face. Most of the girls, when I asked them, agreed readily and promptly scribbled down the address. But I saw a flicker of curiosity cross their faces, as if I was the last person they expected to get such an invitation from . . .

The ward was busy when I arrived for duty. Mr Weaver was sitting in the ward corridor, outside his door. He looked dejected as he watched the frantic activity all around him through his pale, impassive eyes. There had been some kind of pile-up at the roundabout not a hundred yards from the hospital, and Casualty were feeding us up the bloodsplattered, bewildered drivers involved. I bent over Mr Weaver and pulled his dressing gown over his exposed throat.

'You should be in bed, you know. You'll get a cold sitting here.'

'They're moving me.' He looked up at me with his limp smile. 'You got your way, Matron. They're putting me in there.' He nodded towards the main ward.

'You'll be much happier.'

'Will I?'

'You'll have company for a start.'

He shuddered suddenly. 'I'm not seeking company, Matron. I told you that.'

I crouched down next to him. His face looked grey and unshaven. Sister and a porter wheeled another patient through the corridor in front of us, and in the opposite direction Ruth Fullman sped along, pushing a laundry-laden trolley.

'D'you remember I told you I was hoping to move into a new flat?' I said. He swivelled his eyes round to look at me.

'It's a mixed flat in Vauxhall. I've been there about a week now. Before that I always lived on my own . . .'

Elaine, the Auxiliary, swept out of the sluice room opposite. She beamed a greeting at me before waddling off down towards the ward.

'And what's that got to do with me?' Weaver asked.

'Simply that I did it reluctantly, like you moving in there. But in fact . . .' I remembered the supper the night before. The welcoming party they were holding for me. 'It's working out very well. I never thought *I* needed company either, but now I know what I was missing.'

'Spare me your homespun philosophy, Matron.' Weaver looked down the passage towards the main ward. 'I'm not one of your half-witted patients who grab every kind word like a bone. If you're experiencing your first sexual encounter, please accept my congratulations. I did all that some twenty-odd years ago.'

I stared at his undistinguished profile for a moment, then said: 'You're determined not to let anyone help you, aren't you?'

'That's right.'

'But why?'

'Matron.' He turned to look at me. 'I appreciate the thought, but I've explained my reasons for wanting to stay in by myself. Nothing's changed.'

'So you're still expecting the worst. Even though your biopsy result hasn't come through yet?'

He studied me carefully for a second. 'You know why I always call you Matron. Because you're the careful type. The sort who studies for exams weeks ahead. Who always arrives early for appointments. Who does everything by the book. Well, I'm just the opposite. I've never been ready for anything in my life. I've failed everything, every exam I ever sat. Why? Because I never prepared myself for them. The wife walked out on me about ten years ago. You know what I felt?' He threw the question out at me, but continued talking before I could reply. 'Surprised. Not hurt, or particularly upset. Just surprised. I wasn't expecting it. I had been too busy leading my own life to think about her. It's been that way all along. I was unprepared for everything life threw at me. God knows why . . . Well, just this once, I'm going to put the record straight. I'm going to be prepared. And this is the big one, isn't it? The last surprise.' His limp smile returned. 'Except that this time I want to be ready for it. Ready and waiting.'

My knees began to ache and I straightened up. 'I'll walk you to your bed.'

He stood up and pulled his dressing gown around him. 'I can manage.' And with that he slowly shuffled up the corridor towards the ward.

I was too busy that afternoon and evening to think about the party or giving out any more invitations. The new admissions caused a lot of extra work and Sister had to go early, leaving me in charge. It was after ten before I left the ward, with the patients all settled down to sleep and the night nurses safely installed with their instructions.

Half an hour later I quietly let myself into the flat. It was silent and in total darkness, so I assumed everyone was either in bed or out somewhere. I hesitated a moment outside Paul's door, not for any particular reason, but because it had grown into a habit . . . Then I continued up the passage towards my own room. Since there was no one around to talk to, I went straight to bed. I had that intensely weary sort of tiredness that makes you drift off as soon as your head touches the pillow.

It must have been around one a.m. when the voices awoke me. At first they seemed to be some confused extension of my dream, but they grew louder and more detailed until, just for a moment, I thought they were coming from inside my room . . . I shot up in bed, clutching a sheet and listening. It was Paul and Tony, obviously returning from some heavy night out. There was a lot of giggling going on, and surreptitious choking laughter. Tony's voice sounded slurred while Paul's sounded unnaturally hoarse and piercing. They went into the kitchen and I sank back into bed, listening to their giggles. There was a lot of crashing and banging about, immediately followed by a 'Shush!' from one or other of them. Since there wasn't much chance of getting back to sleep, I decided to get up and make us all some coffee. I reached for my dressing gown and pulled it on and was just opening the door when I heard my name mentioned. I didn't know what to do, so I stood there, one hand on the doorknob, listening to them. Paul was talking, but his voice got momentarily lost in the sound of a tap running. Then I heard a chair scrape and Tony said: 'It's only a party, for God's sake. Why all the fuss?'

'Because the poor kid thinks it's in her honour. You didn't have to tell her that, did you?'

'It's true, in a way.' Tony hiccupped slightly. 'Besides, how else are we going to meet them?'

'There must be another way.'

'Look,' Tony said. 'She's been here over a week. And during that time, she's never mentioned a friend. Never had a phone call, no one's called round, nothing. A party is the only solution.'

'And supposing she twigs it?' Paul said. 'What then?'

'She won't,' Tony said confidently. There was a clink of glasses and the slurp of liquid being poured. 'Besides, we've done nothing to be ashamed of. We've given her a room in a damned nice flat, and God knows she's a dull enough creature . . . All we want in return is to meet some nice . . .' – his voice took on a licentious tone – 'sexy little nurses. There must be tons of 'em stuck away in that hospital, all ripe for the plucking.'

The doorknob suddenly felt icy in my hand. I pulled off my dressing gown and crawled into bed. For a while I just lay there, staring at the ceiling, their voices a dim rumble in the back of my head. So that was it. Unanswered questions, questions I'd never really acknowledged until then, suddenly found an outlet and emerged. Those surreptitious glances they'd exchanged when I'd first come to see the flat and they learnt I was a nurse. Paul's odd uneasiness at the mention of the party. It all fell into place. I was simply a means to their ends. The unwitting supplier of nurses to satisfy their adolescent appetites. I turned over and tried to block out the sound of their voices. I didn't feel angry, or even resentful. I simply felt a kind of jaded acceptance. As if the last week, the momentary glimpse into another kind of existence, was now over. I suppose I should have felt disappointed in Paul, yet I didn't. I felt disappointed in myself because I had fallen for the whole thing. Because I had allowed myself to be cheated. Another sort of girl might have got angry, I suppose. She might have gone into the kitchen and demanded explanations. Yet that called for a kind of courage that I simply didn't possess. A sort of self-certainty about oneself and the way one should be treated. I had the odd sensation, lying on my side in that bed, of seeing myself from the viewpoint of others. Such an objective flash of insight is rare and disconcerting. I saw my stolid, plain figure, and my slow and careful mind. I understood, just for a brief moment, why it was that people reacted to me with such restraint and unease. I was the mirror image of their gauche side, the awkward, stumbling side we all have, but manage to cover with a veneer of sophistication. I felt exposed and naked. I lay on my back and shut my eyes. I knew that my guileless days were now over. The flicker of sentiment that Paul had evoked in me had frozen solid. The numbness I felt would gradually wear off and turn into a brief, sharp pain, which in turn would harden into a firm resolve not to repeat the experience.

The following morning I moved out. I heard them all leave the flat, in dribs and drabs, at around nine o'clock. Paul was the last to leave. I heard him prepare breakfast for himself, and then washing in the bathroom. Then the thud of the front door shutting and he was gone. I went to the window and watched him trudge up the road. Then I rang up my old landlady, Mrs Levy. I remembered she'd told me that she was going to have my old room redecorated; with luck it might still be vacant. She was obviously surprised to hear from me, and just a little cagey. Yes, the room was free she said, and yes, I'd be welcome to move back in. There was a little pause, and then she added that of course the rent had increased. The new decorations, inflation . . . She had no choice but to add on three pounds a week. I hung up and looked at myself in the hall mirror. Back to square one. Except, ironically, it would now cost me an extra three pounds a week.

The room was exactly the same. The woodwork, perhaps, had a slight bloom on it, and had evidently been touched up here and there. That doubtless constituted redecoration in the eyes of Mrs Levy. The limp candlewick bedspread still hung over the bed and the faded wallpaper still clung halfheartedly to the walls. Mrs Levy fussed around while I unpacked, flicking a yellow duster over the furniture and watching me with furtive interest.

'You didn't like this new place then?'

'No.'

She started to rub at the bedhead. 'Rent too high, I suppose?'

I turned to face her. I had a sudden desire to shock this small, prying woman. 'They're the kind of people who reckon nurses make an easy lay. You know the sort.'

'You mean ...' She stared at me in horror. 'They didn't try ...?'

'Oh, no.' I smiled wryly. 'It wasn't me they were after. I was simply the contact. The go-between. It was my friends they were after. They hoped to meet lots of dishy nurses through me.'

She looked at me in bewilderment. 'Well I never!'

I was late turning up for duty that afternoon. Sister called to me as I passed her office door.

'Nurse Brent?'

I skidded to a halt and crossed to her. 'Yes, Sister?'

'We've a new admission I'd like you to prepare for theatre. A Mr Frazier. He's for a tracheotomy.'

'Right, Sister.' I started to move off, then stopped. 'Has Mr Weaver got his results through yet?'

'Yes. He's been cleared. He's ready for discharge.' She smiled. 'I relented and let him back into the side ward. He was so miserable in the main ward. He's a funny sort of man ...' She paused for a second. 'When I told him the biopsy result, he didn't say a thing. Just stared at me. Didn't show any emotion at all. Odd, isn't it?'

'Like you say. He's a funny sort of man.'

'Yes ... Anyway, you'd better pop in and see him when you get the chance. He's been asking for you.'

'For me?' I said in surprise.

'And don't forget Mr Frazier,' said Sister, before disappearing into her office.

There was no answer when I tapped on Mr Weaver's side ward door. I'd assumed he wasn't there, when he suddenly opened it for me.

'Well, well. If it isn't Matron.'

'Hello, Mr Weaver.'

'Step inside, said the spider to the fly.' He waved an arm and opened the door wider. I sidled past him. His suitcase was on the bed, with clothes and pyjamas strewn across it.

'Packing?' I asked with a perfunctory smile.

'After a fashion.'

He sat on the bed and looked at me. 'I wanted to say ta for everything before I shoot off.'

'It's been a pleasure. I'm glad things have worked out for you.'

'You heard, then?'

I nodded, and added: 'So you did all that worrying for nothing. You were convinced the results would be positive, weren't you?'

'Yes.' He got up and walked to the window. 'D'you know what I felt when Sister told me?' He turned to face me. 'Cheated. Oh, not sorry. I don't actually want to die. But I'd prepared myself for it, you see. For once in my life, I'd actually prepared myself . . . And then I'm pipped at the post, just like always.'

He was looking at me, his thin lips curled into that limp smile of his.

'Cheated by death. Daft, isn't it?'

I never really understood Mr Weaver when he talked like this, and so an uneasy silence followed. He seemed to notice my uneasiness, because he suddenly rubbed his hands together and walked towards me.

'Anyway, I just wanted to say cheerio. You've been a good girl, listening to all my meanderings. Hope I haven't depressed you too much?'

'Not at all.'

'Good.' He looked at me vaguely and said, 'How's this flat of yours working out?'

'Oh. Not so well, actually. It's proved rather inconvenient, travelling-wise.' I smiled what I hoped was a bright smile. 'So I moved back into my old place.'

'Oh.' He was looking at me intently, his eyes probing my face.

'Besides,' – I crossed to the bed and mechanically started to straighten it – 'I don't think sharing a flat suits me. I'm too used to being on my own.'

'It does grow into a habit.'

'Yes . . .' I straightened up and flashed him another smile. 'Well, I'm so glad you're all right, Mr Weaver. Do pop in and see us sometime, won't you?' And with that standard nurse/patient farewell, I made for the door. I just had it open when his voice whipped out at me.

'Funny, really.'

I turned back to him expectantly. He smiled, revealing the nicotine-stained teeth.

'We've both been cheated, haven't we?'

'What makes you think I've been cheated, Mr Weaver?' I asked with dignity.

He walked back to the window and leant on the sill, staring out at the Park beyond.

'Because it takes one to know one, Matron. That's why.'

St. Angela's Hospital

MERICI ROAD
LONDON S.W. 11

**HOSPITAL SCHOOL OF NURSING
CONFIDENTIAL REPORT**

Surname Fullman **Forenames** Ruth Claire

Date of birth 5/11/55 **Expected date of final examination** Autumn 1975

Previous nursing or other relevant qualifications None

Confidential report

Ruth Fullman is now well into her third year of training. She is a capable, practical girl, with a thorough grasp of nursing and nursing procedures. During her three years she has come to accept the disciplines of nursing and carry out her duties efficiently. She does, however, have a tendency to speak her mind; this sometimes leads to friction with the senior nurses. There is an impetuous streak in her which has, in the past, put her into awkward situations.

Heather Windrup

Heather Windrup, Senior Nursing Tutor

RUTH While Shirley moved back into her old home, Ruth was leaving her parents' home vowing never to return to it. She had spent the past week on holiday in the Yorkshire town where she was born and where her mother and stepfather still lived in a street of terrace houses called Daisy Street. Daisy Street had always been neat and plain, but now, since the local council had banned cars from it and had landscaped tiny gardens at intervals along the pavements, it was neat and pretty. She had slept in the back bedroom she had first shared with her sister Carole, eventually, when Carole left home, knowing the heady joy of having it all to herself. She had stood looking through the bedroom window across the street to the row of exactly similar houses opposite, remembering a boy called Frank Mullen who used to make dates with her by writing time and place on a child's blackboard and holding it up at his own bedroom window. Frank was in Canada now teaching Indian children and probably never giving Ruth a second's thought. And she had said hello to the neighbours, like Mrs Harrison who had had seven operations and believed, possibly with some justification, that she knew more about hospitals than Ruth ever would; also old Joe Mason in the bottom house, who never wore a coat and could still not be trusted alone with women though he would be seventy-one next birthday. Then there were the young newly-weds at number sixteen, who went everywhere holding hands and shopped together at the local supermarket every Thursday evening, a fact which never ceased to amaze Ruth's mother, whose husband disdained shopping as woman's work.

It should have been a pleasant week, a rest, a chance to relax among familiar faces and places, thought Ruth, as she waited at the station for the train to take her back to London and St Angela's. Instead she felt more tense and miserable than she had a week ago when, tired and somewhat disillusioned by overwork and a wage which despite recent rises was still derisively inadequate, she had arrived home rather like a harassed fox seeking the peace and sanctuary of its den. Some den! she mused ruefully. More of a madhouse.

'Pardon?' asked her sister Carole, who was waiting with her.

'H'mm?' said Ruth, still reflecting on the disasters and traumas of the past week.

'Thought you spoke.'

'No'.

They both lapsed into silence, hardly a companionable one either. Ruth's troubles at home were mainly caused by friction between herself and her mother, but Carole was a component of that friction, albeit an innocent one.

It was Carole who broke the silence. 'Had a rotten time, haven't you, kid?' she said.

'You could say that,' replied Ruth.

'How do you think I feel having to live there?' said Carole, bitterness sharpening her usually pleasant voice.

'I don't envy you for a second,' said Ruth.

'I bet you don't,' said Carole. 'And I'll tell you something. Hard as you think it is. Tired as you get. Browned-off as you get. I'd still give anything to be going back to St Angela's instead of you. Anything!' And she said it with such vehemence that her normally placid brown eyes for a moment caught fire.

A bell clattered in a nearby office and almost immediately there was the faint rattling sound of an approaching train. Carole bent to the yellow pram at her side and spoke to the child lying in it, quietly sucking a fat thumb. 'Puff-puff's coming, love. Don't you want to see it? 'Course you do.' She lifted the child out of the pram, holding it in her arms and indicating the track to their left. 'Look up there for the puff-puff, Susan,' she said. 'Look up there for the puff-puff.' But Susan was much more interested in her Auntie Ruth and the gaggle of passengers also waiting for the train. Several of the passengers made no secret of a similar interest in her, for Susan was a beautiful child. She was also coloured.

Comfortable in a window seat, if sometimes a trifle worried by the train's speed, Ruth watched England darting past her. She registered very little of it apart from the more dramatic landmarks: a canal with coloured boats on it; a motorway suddenly writhing alongside for a minute and then vanishing as if it had been severed; a chemical plant, all knitted steel pipes and ladders and sinister gases curling from odd corners. But they were staccato images in what was largely a blur, unlike the mental pictures which obsessed her, images of home, and her mother and Carole and little Susan, whose affectionate goodbye kiss was still slightly sticky on her cheek.

Dear bonny little Susan, thought Ruth as the train slashed through a station; her good looks and sunny personality were in direct contradiction to her uncertain future. Uncertain not just because she was coloured, which however much attitudes may be changing is still a formidable handicap in the world as it is, and certainly in England as it is. But besides that, Susan had no father, or, putting it another way, her mother had no husband, not living with her anyway. The Nigerian engineering student Carole had married had gone back to his own country to work before Susan was born, promising to send for them both as soon as he had saved up enough money, but never communicating another single solitary word. All that Carole had heard, through a Nigerian girl she had met in training (for Carole too had been a nurse), was that he was alive and working extremely hard in some remote town in the interior.

A fat man reading the *Guardian* across the compartment distracted Ruth. His rheumy eyes would appear above his newspaper, ogle her for a second and then vanish again like a jack-in-the-box. The next time they appeared she froze him with a stare of such cold scorn that he not only retreated behind his paper hardly to appear again but also seemed to contract physically in his seat. She was good at that sort of thing, was Ruth, and she rather enjoyed it, too. Her square, nice face with its regular features, which in the right mood and circumstances could be very beautiful, belied a steely personality.

Was that her trouble, she wondered, her mind in a turmoil again. Was she too inflexible? Was she herself perhaps to blame for her mother's antagonism and bitterness? Was not her mother right to be suspicious and frightened for Ruth after what she had seen happen to Carole? Was it not very natural she should look upon a nursing career as a helter-skelter to shame and sorrow? Especially somebody with a working-class background like hers, with its rigid code of right and wrong and a self-respect which had to be defended to the death and particularly against the neighbours.

She could have been more understanding, thought Ruth ruefully, tried to argue her case to her mother instead of stating dogmatically that nothing in the world would stop her becoming a nurse. For all Ruth cared, Carole could have got herself into trouble with half a dozen assorted cannibals. She was going to be a nurse because she wanted to be a nurse more than anything and her mother could rant and rave and sulk till doomsday, she would not change her mind. And anyway she had more commonsense than her sister. *She* would never throw herself at the first handsome man, black or white, who breathed aftershave in her ear. She wanted a career, not marriage, and, as far as she was concerned, men were merely part of the social scene to be courted and discarded according to whim.

Ruth smiled to herself as she recalled her mother's reaction to that last statement. 'If you believe that, my girl,' she said, 'you're either a fool or a bitch. And I don't think you're a bitch. So you must be a fool then, who's just as capable of jumping into bed and being caught out as the millions of other little fools there are in the world. So don't talk rubbish to me, love. At least don't insult my intelligence by doing that.' Her mother, for all her starchy morality and devotion to clean underwear, could be startlingly forthright at times.

But she had failed to weaken Ruth's resolve and she had watched her daughter pack her suitcase and leave to start her training at St Angela's with resentment pinching the corners of her mouth and her heart, already soured, turning to stone. She had lost her first husband from cancer at thirty-two and had remarried only to discover that love, like lightning, does not strike in the same place twice. She had seen her eldest daughter contract a marriage that was inconceivable. She had endured the twitching curtains, the severed whispers, the muted excitement of relatives and friends scenting an even grander scandal when Susan arrived and her daddy disappeared. And now her younger daughter was embarking on the same journey which to her could have only one possible catastrophic end.

Poor mum, thought Ruth. Poor, poor mum! I should be shot, I should be bloody well shot! The train pulled into King's Cross with the usual hiccup, which she was pleased to see caught the fat man with the *Guardian* off-balance and sent him reeling down the passageway all confusion and sweaty embarrassment. Ruth got up, retrieved her own suitcase, left the train and walked along the platform to the exit with a heavy heart and the beginnings of a headache lurking just above her right eye.

Jo said cheerfully when she walked into the flat they shared, 'You're in for it. Are you in for it!'

'Eh?' queried Ruth, flopping into an elderly cane chair. She felt barely alive after the journey through London, her headache swelling with every thud of a tube-train door and every frantic scurry from choked train to choked platform to choked street.

'I said you're in for it,' repeated Jo, obviously relishing her role of Cassandra.

'Am I?' said Ruth, kicking off her shoes.

'The whole hospital has gone barmy. There's only twenty-two nurses off sick with some sort of food bug! *And* they've closed the nurses' home kitchen till they trace what it is. So everything they eat has to come from outside and quite often it doesn't. So they're all browned-off. And Jill Palmer came off nights with me Monday morning and hasn't been seen since and the police have been told. I think she's trying to get a job singing, well you know how she fancies she's got a voice. Which she hasn't. And . . . no, I think that's all, actually. Except everybody's run off their feet and there's only been me and Staff on Men's Surgical all week, well, since Jill scarpered.'

'Thanks very much,' said Ruth flatly, 'that's all I need.' She thought it might be nice to die sitting there, and pass gently into oblivion and everlasting peace like an old aunt of hers who had died in her chair, reading Ethel M. Dell.

'Not had such a good time up in the tundra?' asked Jo, though she was not really interested. She was on duty in half an hour and was engaged in the usual frenzied last-minute dash to wash, clean her teeth, dress, clean her shoes, do her face, brush her hair, describe her current boyfriend, all at one and the same time, which was rather like a threshing machine going into action.

Jo was as disorganized as Ruth was organized and, though Ruth hated it, she was wise enough to realize that she would be lonely in the flat without Jo and even more introspective, especially at the moment.

'No, I didn't have a good time,' she confided.

'Your mum cut up rough again, did she?' queried Jo dutifully, as she slipped into her coat and grabbed an apple for the bus journey.

'Who else?'

'How's your sister and the baby?'

'Well . . . Carole's . . . well, you know, in her situation. Susan's fine. A real bonny girl.'

'That's something.'

'Yeah.'

'Right then,' said Jo. 'I'm off. See you when you come on in the morning. But if I don't . . . best of luck. You'll need it.'

And she went to work, leaving Ruth staring glumly into space and wondering if she should catch the next train back home, make it up with her mother, and settle for an office job somewhere local and later perhaps marry a nice clean Yorkshire lad who would tip up his wage willingly every Friday and be a marvellous father to her three kids. She closed her eyes, blotting out the image because she knew it was false to her character and to her ambition. Perhaps some day she might return to Yorkshire but tomorrow was for St Angela's and whatever rough times Jo had forecast.

Actually Ruth felt much better when she went on to the ward the next morning. Male Medical seemed bright and cheerful and the patients' flowers made vivid splashes of colour, especially those that stood in the sun. She gave each of its nineteen denizens a quick glance of appraisal and a cheerful 'Good morning' as she sought out copies of the *Daily Mail* and *Daily Mirror* to read during her coffee break. It was one of the perks to take over discarded newspapers and magazines and Ruth, always an avid reader, took full advantage of it. During one quiet Sunday night she had read five newspapers from cover to cover, apart from the sports pages, and found herself totally confused, particularly about the political scene.

Many of the patients in the ward were familiar to her, like the young schoolboy, Michael Fish, who had damaged his back in an accident in the gymnasium and was on traction. 'Still keeping you out of mischief, are we, Michael?' she asked him and he grinned and blushed as he always did when a nurse spoke to him, even Mavis Grant who was beginning to grow a moustache.

In the next bed was Mr Riley, who was lying on top of the bed-clothes in his dressing gown, his eyes closed as though fast asleep. A small lively man of fifty-eight, he was having bladder trouble and was in for tests. 'Dreaming of all the beer you've not been able to drink lately, Mr Riley?' said Ruth, knowing full well that he was not asleep for he found it difficult to rest and had to be knocked out with sleeping pills every night.

His eyes flicked open instantly and he said, 'What do you fancy at Haydock today?'

'Red Knees in the three o'clock,' replied Ruth. 'Can't lose.'

During the fortnight or so he had been in hospital, Mr Riley had taken it upon himself to educate Ruth in matters of the turf and Ruth had responded willingly enough, particularly when she discovered she quite often struck lucky, winning small amounts with small each-way bets while Mr Riley complained that he lost hundreds of pounds, which she did not really believe because, for one thing, both his slippers had holes in the soles.

'Red Knees,' he scoffed, 'hasn't got a cat in hell's chance, it's a donkey.'

'I'm prepared to put my money where my mouth is; can't do more than that,' said Ruth loftily and she passed on down the ward leaving Mr Riley scowling after her.

It was then she noticed a new patient in the end bed, a very handsome Sunday-supplement sort of man with flecks of grey at his dark temples and teeth like milk and wearing very expensive pyjamas, the collar of which showed neatly above his very expensive dark-blue dressing gown. She smiled at him, and he smiled back. She felt slightly silly and girlish, which was unusual for someone normally as collected as Ruth. All the way back up the ward she was sure she could feel his eyes on her and she worried if her cap was on straight and whether he had noticed that she was slightly knock-kneed.

Ruth's interest in the new patient was short-lived. Sister Rothwell announced, not without some satisfaction, that Staff and Ruth comprised the entire nursing complement for that day. Two student nurses were down with the bug and a third was having a minor operation on a bone in her foot which had been slowly cracking up under the strain of walking a million miles a day. Ruth groaned inwardly at the news. The routine million miles would be multiplied at least three times and her own feet were hardly rugged. At the end of a normal day it often seemed as if all feeling finished at her ankles and her feet had turned to stone. Sister made light of it, her round face beaming because she was the sort who saw overwork as a challenge to be overcome by cheery exhortations like. 'Shoulders to the wheel, eh nurse?' or even 'Up, up and away we go!', delivered in a near hysterical falsetto. 'She'd go far in the Brownies,' Jo had once observed with sarcasm.

The day gradually gained momentum until it became a general blur of meals, bedmaking, dressings, pills, baths, Sister's shrill voice and whirlwind visits from the Houseman, a certain lusting Doctor Carter, against whom rumour had it, even steel knickers were not proof. He only ever seemed to work with one hand – the other was usually snaked round the nearest nurse's waist. Ruth did manage to discover that the new patient's name was Mr Young and she exchanged a few more smiles with him, but he was away most of the morning in X-Ray and she never actually got to speak to him. It was when she was giving him his lunch that they exchanged their first words.

'Busy day,' he said, making it a statement rather than an inquiry.

'You can say that again,' said Ruth, whipping the cover off his chop and chips and handing him the plate.

'What's that?' he asked, indicating the meat.

'A chop, I think,' said Ruth.

'There hasn't been a fire in the kitchen, has there?' he said, his eyes smiling as much as his mouth.

What a charming man, thought Ruth, responding to him immediately, her advancing fatigue abruptly halted. Agreeable people, like time and pleasant landscapes, are splendid healers.

'Actually the chef has been in prison for arson,' she said, repeating a well-used hospital joke.

'I can believe it,' said Mr Young.

Ruth passed on with the lunch trolley, wondering how old he was and making a mental note to find out from his case-notes and also to discover why he was in hospital. He looked healthy enough, fairly tanned as all handsome men should be, and he possessed a normal appetite, she noted, covertly watching him dissect the overcooked chop and eat it not without some relish. But she forgot her queries as she instantly became embroiled in a minor drama with old Mr Portman, who began to have trouble with his breathing as he did quite often, and had to be put on oxygen. Sister Rothwell herself trundled in the oxygen cylinder at a terrific pace, singing out as she swept up the ward, 'Here come the Marines!'

She's barmy, thought Ruth, and exchanged an amused glance with Mr Young, who plainly shared her opinion of Sister Rothwell. Sister already had the mask on Mr Portman's face and was saying to him, 'Come along, Mr Portman, breathe deeply now, we'll soon have you fighting fit.' For all the world as if he were a new recruit on an assault course instead of an old man who would probably be dead within the week. Still, thought Ruth, indulging herself with one of her introspective moments, Sister's breeziness was all part of the psychology of hospitals, which require a certain pitch of boisterous insensitivity and ruthlessness to survive. Without their Sister Rothwells, they would very likely sink into a state of deep melancholia, weary with trying to defeat sickness and death which, like greed, never can be defeated finally.

Ruth discovered why Mr Young was in hospital when Sister Rothwell used a brief lull in the activity just after lunch to discuss the condition of certain patients. Not one for wasting even a second was Sister Rothwell. Apparently he had lost the sight of one eye, and a heart murmur had also been diagnosed; but after four days' complete rest his sight had returned and his heart condition was now being investigated. 'Nothing organically wrong with the eye,' observed Sister, 'so it was probably the body letting him know he was abusing it. He looks a bit of a Champagne Charlie, don't you think, probably gallivanting about drinking and doing the Lord knows what until all hours. Eh, Nurse Fullman?'

The question was rhetorical really, but Ruth found herself suddenly blushing and springing to Mr Young's defence. 'Oh I don't know, Sister,' she said. 'He seems a nice man. Probably overworked.'

'Overworked!' sniffed Sister. 'Work never killed anybody. Certainly not nurses – if it did I'd have been dead long since and look at me. Fit as a fiddler's elbow and strong as an ox.' And she looks it, thought Ruth, noting Sister Rothwell's strong square shoulders, billowing bosom and legs like pillars. Ruth wondered if she bullied her husband and decided that she must do. She would treat him like a patient and he in turn would treat her like a ward sister.

Ruth did not speak to Mr Young again that day because the pace quickly picked up again and she was engaged with a couple of pre-ops and another minor emergency with Mr Portman, who, it was discovered, had not peed all day and had to be persuaded, with some difficulty, to try to do so; he eventually did. She did notice Mr Young, however, helping Staff to collect the afternoon teacups, which seemed to confirm her favourable assessment of him.

Jo was still in bed when she got back to the flat, so, true to custom, Ruth rattled a spoon in a pan till she wakened, groaning that she felt sick, that life was nothing but bed and work and had Raoul rung?

'Who?' asked Ruth.

'Raoul,' grimaced Jo, sitting up in bed and trying to scratch her back and her kneecap at one and the same time, which made her look rather grotesque.

'Raoul!' said Ruth dismissively as if the name itself explained everything, which to her it did. In her opinion Western Europe was decadent and acquisitive. Her hero was Tito like her father's before her and she wished that Aneurin Bevan had lived to become Prime Minister instead of Harold Wilson whom she could not stand.

'He's French, he's on holiday and his dad's something posh in the French Foreign Office and I told you about him yesterday,' said Jo, getting out of bed and stretching so hard that her small breasts seemed in danger of bursting her white skin. 'Oh and he's lovely and I think I'm going to make a fool of myself over him,' she added.

'Won't be the first time, will it?' sniffed Ruth, taking her shoes off and feeling her feet just to make sure she still had any.

'Oh, one of those days, was it?' said Jo, belatedly detecting the fatigue and depression in Ruth's voice. 'Don't say I didn't warn you. Who was on the ward with you?'

'Sister and Staff.'

'Busy, were you?'

'You could say that.'

'Poor you.'

'I thought you might have had a meal ready.'

'Ah .. well,' said Jo, plainly embarrassed though not overmuch because she could be quite self-centred, especially where her love life was concerned. 'I'm meeting Raoul for a meal before I go to work. Well, a snack anyway. So I don't really want anything now,' she added lamely.

Ruth never got round to making a meal that night either. For one thing she was too tired to do so and for another they had nothing in the flat that she particularly wanted to eat. One thing about going home, she got plenty of food. Her mother was an excellent plain cook, her steak and kidney pie, roast potatoes, mashed swedes and carrots making that rare thing, a perfectly balanced dish. Compared with grub like that, tinned spaghetti on toast or sliced beef in a pallid plastic bag seemed an insult to the palate and certainly to the stomach. She did not sleep very well, either, for her feet were aching and her mind again churning over the problems of her mother and sister and herself till it became a solid weight pressing her into the pillow and threatening to stifle her. She got up and opened the window but that just let in the sound of the traffic so she had to close it again.

Sister Rothwell noticed the inevitable results of a sleepless night immediately. 'Out on the tiles last night, were we, Nurse Fullman?' she said, jocularly enough but Ruth was hardly amused. 'Never mind, nothing like hard work for clearing the brain and sharpening the reflexes. Best foot forward for me,

Matron and Barbara Castle, eh, Nurse? Oh, and not forgetting the patients! But just don't let me catch you giving yourself a boost with a whiff of Mr Portman's oxygen. It can get to be a habit.'

Mr Young was rather more tactful when she gave him his breakfast. 'Not feeling up to par, Nurse?' he asked gently.

'I'm fine,' she replied, wishing she had done more with her face and perhaps hidden most of the dark rings under her eyes and the slight puffiness round the cheekbones.

'You look tired,' he persisted, again gently.

'Occupational hazard,' she said. 'Yours *was* a boiled egg?'

He nodded and Ruth moved on to the next bed but all the way round the ward she knew without a shadow of doubt that he was watching her and the certainty pleased her. Also it suddenly struck her that Mr Young bore a marked physical resemblance to her own father, especially as he looked in a cherished photograph taken just before he died. Her spirits, however, soon dived to rock bottom again as the morning's labours crowded in on her and Mr Portman took a turn for the worse. The orthopaedic consultant was plainly unhappy with young Michael's back, and Staff had a blazing row with Sister Rothwell about smoking in the kitchen which left them both sulky and tending to take their ill temper out on poor Ruth.

Mr Young caught Ruth sitting in Sister's office apparently checking the workbook but actually snatching a few minutes' rest. 'Port in a storm?' he queried, those white teeth of his flashing on cue.

'You must be a mind reader,' said Ruth, smiling in her turn.

'Actually I'm an architect. Well, a local government architect, which isn't quite Coventry Cathedral standard but we do have rather a nice line in bus shelters.' He said it with such disarming candour, without a trace of self-denigration, like a man content with his own place in the world, that Ruth's first impressions were definitely confirmed. She liked the man, he put her at ease. He seemed genuine, he was considerate and he obviously had a sense of humour.

'An architect,' repeated Ruth, because that was all she could think of to say.

'How long have you been a nurse?' he asked. 'Not long, I bet.'

'Seems like *too* long . . . well, today anyway,' said Ruth ruefully. 'This is my third year.'

'Don't know how you've stuck it. After what . . . five days in here I'm agog with admiration for your profession. Where do you get the energy from? It would kill a docker to work at the pace you do. It would, he'd be dead before his first tea-break.'

'What about architects?'

'Oh, we don't work, we just design structures that are unsuitable for what they're supposed to do, like high-rise flats.'

'You've got to have the brains.'

'No, just an ability to pass exams, which is not the same thing, as Mr Churchill would no doubt have testified. Seems to me nurses have brains and energy and commonsense, a very rare combination indeed. Plus good looks.'

'You'll be having me blushing,' said Ruth, feeling the blood in her cheeks already.

'And you do it beautifully,' said Mr Young, managing to make the words natural instead of corny as ninety-nine men out of a hundred would have done. At least that was how they sounded to Ruth. But then in her low state of morale she was vulnerable to flattery.

Sister walked in then and joshed Mr Young for taking up Ruth's time. 'Now, now, Mr Young,' she said, 'we can't have this. Patients are patients and nurses are nurses and never the twain shall meet except in bed, if you'll pardon the expression. So will you please return to yours.'

'Willingly, Sister,' grinned Mr Young, 'if I'm to meet you in it.'

'Oh, Mr Young,' simpered Sister with exaggerated skittishness. 'The things you men say!'

Mr Young left the office, winking ever so slightly at Ruth as he did so, but not slightly enough to escape Sister's beady eye. She said, when Mr Young had gone, 'Nice man, Mr Young, which means he wants watching. Do you know what his christian name is?'

'No,' said Ruth, who didn't because she had not yet had the opportunity to look at his case-notes.

'Ashley,' said Sister, 'Ashley Young, which makes him even more dangerous, don't you think? Oh and he doesn't get on with his wife, either. At least, that's my opinion and I'm not often wrong. Well I don't miss much, do I? Like now for instance . . .'

'Sister . . . ?' queried Ruth, all innocence.

'You're slacking, Nurse, shirking, skulking in here when the action's out there, on the ward.' But there was no note of censure in her voice and she added, just a mite wearily because Sister Rothwell would not have admitted substantial weariness had she been obliged to run the ward singlehanded and nonstop for a month, 'Mind you, I can't altogether blame you for taking a breather after the sort of day you're having, but neither can I say I *can't* blame you, can I? Well, not officially. So chop, chop, Nurse, there's a hundred and one things to do, just like there will be tomorrow and all the other tomorrows I shouldn't wonder! God didn't rest on the seventh day at all, you know. He created the nurse to clean up some of the mess he'd made earlier in the week! And that's the Gospel according to Sylvia Rothwell.'

It was visiting that afternoon and Ruth found herself growing more and more intrigued by the prospect, a feeling almost of excitement which was not even diminished by Jo phoning to say that she would not be in for tea again as she was seeing Raoul, and that Frenchmen really were much more polished, sophisticated and tender than your average Match-of-the-Day English boys. Ruth kept wondering what Mrs Young would be like, and, with absolutely no evidence or justification, pictured her as either dowdy or vulgar or bitchy or possibly all three.

Mrs Young in fact was a beautiful woman, small perhaps but with a figure assembled in exactly the right proportions and maintained in showroom condition. Her face with its high cheekbones and crown of raven hair had a Latin look. She was dressed for the weather in a dark blue vest top, slacks and yellow clogs, and as she moved through the ward even Mr Portman seemed to stop his asthmatic rasping long enough to notice her and perhaps to feel that if he had to carry a last image of the world into the hereafter, she would do very nicely thank you.

It was Mr Portman who supplied Ruth with an excuse to go on the ward during visiting. He complained that the back of his bald head felt sore, so Sister told her to rub some cold cream on it. She drew the curtains round his bed but left a chink through which, if she craned her neck, she could just see Mr Young and his wife. She got the impression, more from Mr Young's face than his wife's, that they were arguing. He was plainly scowling and making the occasional angry gesture with his hand, but she looked either impassive or bland, Ruth was not sure which.

Visiting time ended and the ward once again became Sister's domain. Sister Rothwell hated visitors. They made the place look untidy, interrupted her beloved routine and if she had had her way they would long ago have been banned.

Ruth began the chore of temperature- and pulse-taking, a task she normally loathed, but today she embarked upon it quite cheerfully. When she reached Mr Young he still had a long face and in response to her bright and breezy, 'Open wide,' he just did so without a word. His temperature was normal but his pulse rate had quickened, not alarmingly but enough to warrant a comment. 'Are you feeling all right, Mr Young?' Ruth asked.

'Why?' he queried petulantly.

'Your pulse is up, nothing to worry about really, but . . .?'

He did not let her finish the sentence. He interrupted, looking stonily at her, petulance also showing in the droop of his mouth, 'You should see my wife about it, Nurse. She upsets me rather, doesn't she, sometimes deliberately.'

Ruth was taken aback. It seemed such a childish outburst and so out of character. She found herself staring at him open-mouthed and it took an effort of will to fill in his chart, return it to its place at the foot of the bed and leave him to his ill-humour. She felt cheated, let down, and it was almost a relief to see Doctor Carter descend on them again. At least she knew exactly where she was with him, on the defensive, well physically anyway as he pretended to discuss Mr Portman with her, his hand all the while surreptitiously trying to massage her spine, with Ruth shuffling and swaying like a boxer trying to escape it. He also asked her for a date, but she refused because she found young doctors generally hard to take. They were either extroverts like Paul Carter or they bored you to death with their everlasting jargon and their arrogant conviction that they knew better than anyone else about any subject under the sun and particularly about medicine. God knows where all the Doctor Kildares went to, thought Ruth, as she stalked Doctor Carter round the ward making sure he neither 'borrowed' any equipment like scissors or the ophthalmoscope, nor mislaid case-notes which he was in the habit of leaving behind on a patient's bed. There was a story that several patients had been discovered in a state of severe shock after finding them and reading that the indigestion which they thought they had was actually a form of cancer. With Doctor Carter's departure her shift was suddenly over and she was back in the real world of bus queues and inconsiderate people and an empty flat, and the tinned spaghetti that she hadn't been able to face the previous night.

She had to face it eventually because Jo had scoffed all the beef slices and there was nothing else in the cupboard apart from fish paste which her mother would never even have allowed in the house. But it was not her mother she thought about as she toyed with her spaghetti, one eye on Ray Langton on the ancient black and white telly for which they had no licence. She considered Mr Young, Ashley Young, and the way you can never tell with people. They were always proving her wrong. Carole, for instance, had been a complete surprise. Apparently so gentle and shy, timid even, she had embarked on her love affair with her Nigerian with total certainty and confidence. 'You're as bold as brass,' her mother had accused her, 'like a tart.' And not without some justification. There was her stepfather, too, a good solid man on the surface, yet with a gift for self-deception that was frightening. He would spend half his wage in one night in the railwaymen's club and then complain the rest of the week that he never had the price of a pint. How can you ever trust somebody enough to marry them? mused Ruth. How indeed! She slept like a log that night because her body was exhausted enough to over-rule her brain and insist upon the rest it craved – which was perhaps as well.

Things improved the next day. The two student nurses were back at work and Sister Rothwell had the day off. Sister Francis, a tiny middleaged coloured woman who rarely seemed to speak yet ran everything like clockwork, replaced her. It felt almost like being on holiday to Ruth, who had time to do jobs properly instead of having to cut corners to save precious minutes. She even had time to linger over her coffee in the canteen and listen to Julie Ward's latest escapade. Julie was what the newspapers call fun-loving. Her life was a succession of episodes which would have earned most people at least severe censure or even dismissal but not Julie. Even Sister Tutor, stern as a prison door normally, found it impossible to sustain disapproval for long when confronted by Julie's bright cheeky face with its enormous child's eyes. This time she had been giving the women in Female Surgical 'pregnancy tests' which consisted of suspending a needle on a piece of cotton over the women's stomachs. If the needle revolved to the right they were pregnant, if to the left they were not. The ward was in an uproar, patients without stitches laughing and even those with stitches tittering when Mr Cooper, the consultant surgeon, walked in and laughed louder than anyone, as he usually did.

Ruth also had time to talk to Mr Young. In fact he helped her to make the beds, insisted upon it, and after a couple of false starts, did it very well. She was deliberately cool with him and he obviously realized it, because as soon as they were working with a definite rhythm he said, 'I'm sorry about yesterday.'

'Sorry?' replied Ruth, pretending ignorance, though she knew perfectly well what he was referring to. 'What about?'

'I had no business to be rude to you just because I was . . . well, upset,' he said, again with a directness that rang absolutely true.

'Rude . . . I don't remember you being rude, Mr Young.'

'I was. And the name's Ashley . . . Ruth.'

He held her eyes long enough for her to feel stupidly girlish again and almost to forget his petulance and his temperamental outburst of yesterday; but Ruth was partly defensive, remembering Sister Rothwell's warning.

It was when they were making their fifth bed that he brought up the incident again. He said, as he deftly turned the sheets under the mattress, 'I'm afraid it's the old, old story.'

'Hmm?' queried Ruth, straining to keep pace with him and feeling slightly aggrieved.

'My marriage . . . we're incompatible. June – that's my wife . . . we're incompatible, June and I.'

'I'm sorry,' said Ruth truthfully. It seemed a terrible waste that Ashley Young should have a bad marriage.

'In fact I rather think that's half my trouble.'

'Trouble?'

'My ticker and whatever it was wrong with my eye. Tension and all that, the twentieth-century version of the plague.'

'Your wife's very attractive.'

'She is. We just don't get on.'

'Have you any children?'

'No, thank God.'

They fell silent as they finished the bed, Ruth arranging the pillows in the prescribed order, and moved on to the next where Mr Riley was studying an assortment of racing pages. He had to be coerced into getting up, complaining that they were interrupting his calculations which could cost him thousands of pounds. As a punishment he would never give Ruth another tip. 'I'd be better off for that,' she called after him and Mr Riley responded by giving her the V-sign behind his back.

'So you're a punter, are you?' asked Mr Young.

'Only now and again. I seem to be lucky.'

'Just remember, there are no poor bookmakers.'

'So my father used to say.'

'It's true.'

Again Ruth had to concentrate hard to keep pace with him. He said, 'I don't suppose you're married.'

'No.'

'Engaged?'

'No.'

'Wise girl.'

They worked on in companionable silence, he occasionally smiling at her and Ruth smiling back. She felt as if she had known him for years instead of a mere few hours. Then he said suddenly, 'Of course I'm going to have to do something, or . . . well, I'll be back in here, won't I?'

'Do something?' asked Ruth, puzzled.

'About my marriage.'

'Oh.'

'End it I suppose, though . . . well, that's part of the trouble. June's so demanding, yet so dependent. Shrieking at me one minute, saying she can't live without me the next. It's like living with two different people, neither of them very pleasant. Still, I'm sure you don't want to hear about my problems. I suppose your life's very well regulated – devoted to your job, no time to get too involved with people and their hang-ups.'

'You must be joking,' said Ruth, recalling last week's battles with her mother and how unhappy they had made her.

'You look so . . . so serene.'

'It's the uniform. I'm not really.'

'You'll have to tell me your troubles some time.'

It was a perfectly flat statement, spoken without any nuance or archness but Ruth instinctively knew that he was extending their relationship, extending it beyond that of nurse and patient. He was suggesting that they should take it outside the ward, outside the hospital, into the real world, and she was glad, though still a little doubtful.

'Yes,' she said, 'perhaps I will.'

The next two days were not quite so enjoyable from a work point of view because Sister Rothwell was back whirring away in top gear and doing her cheerleader bit with more gusto than ever. 'I think she's on bloody benzedrine,' groaned Staff. 'I do, I think she's on bloody benzedrine.' But Ruth was in the sort of mood Sister Rothwell could only bruise, never crush. It was a self-satisfied mood, a cat-in-the-creamery mood, a feeling that tomorrow was going to be marvellous no matter what. She slept better, ate better and home and its problems assumed their proper distance which was precisely one hundred and ninety-eight miles away. She talked with Ashley, for that was who he was now. Not often and not for long, but enough. She witnessed a couple more tiffs with his wife and again felt pleased though guilty as well. And their bedmaking became a sort of competition to see who could do his or her bit most quickly: Ruth giggled a lot which caused Sister Rothwell to observe acidly, 'If you were his doctor, Nurse, you'd be halfway to being reported to the General Medical Council for unprofessional conduct.'

Jo gave Ruth a funny look when she got home to the flat that evening. She had a meal prepared, too, only sausage and mash to be sure, but for Jo that was a major culinary achievement. She had it on the table in no time, moreover, and peremptorily told Ruth to sit down and eat it or it would go cold.

'You sound like my mother,' said Ruth, doing as she was told, for she was hungry for the umpteenth time that day.

'Do I?' replied Jo, managing to get a wealth of meaning into two syllables.

They ate, Ruth with relish, Jo slowly because she was constantly casting what could only be described as disapproving glances at her friend. When she could stand it no longer, Ruth asked, 'All right, what am I supposed to have done?'

Jo was in like a flash. 'What's all this I hear,' she said, her voice positively brusque, like a schoolteacher's, 'about you mucking around with a married feller – again?' There was just a slight pause before her final word, just enough to give it an extra edge.

Ruth looked at Jo for a second, her mouth working on a particularly tenacious piece of pork sausage. She swallowed it, then continued her meal as if Jo had never spoken.

'I thought you'd rotten well learned your lesson,' persisted Jo, who had now put down her knife and fork in order to devote all her attention to Ruth. 'How long is it since Frank, two months at the most and here you go again! But in case you've forgotten, if you want proof, I'll show you where you chewed your pillowslip to ribbons if you like. What is it about married fellers? They're dead trouble, Ruth, and you know it.'

Ruth ate stolidly on, not even looking up at Jo, who tried another tack. 'Is it all a load of rubbish what that silly bitch Julie Wood was saying? I mean, she's putting it about you've been all but drawing his curtains round and jumping into bed with this bloke. Well, you know Julie. If you lend a doctor your biro, you're having it off with him. So it's not true, is it?'

Ruth popped the last bit of sausage into her mouth.

'Ruth!' said Jo, getting angry.

Ruth got rid of this piece rather more quickly, then she looked at Jo and said calmly, 'I'll tell you what's true, Jo, I *like* Ashley...'

'Ashley!' repeated Jo, as if she could not quite believe anyone could possibly be called Ashley.

'I like him a lot,' continued Ruth. 'And it's my business, so let's drop the subject before we fall out and one of us has to pack her bags. What's for afters?'

'Tinned prunes,' said Jo and she went into the kitchenette to get them, because she knew Ruth well enough to understand that the subject was closed and to pursue it would be to invite a major row which she was not prepared to risk. Like Ruth she realized that in some ways they were opposites and, like Ruth, she knew that despite this they were good for each other. She just hoped with all her heart that Ruth would not get involved with this man. Despite her clear-headedness, her hardness, her strong principles, she could be an awful fool about men. Jo could not quite put it into words, but she suspected Ruth tended to use men as a form of escape, and when the pressures were strongest the need to escape was strong, too. And that was when she was most vulnerable, like now.

Ruth scoffed at Jo's strictures as she lay in bed that night. Cheek of her, she thought. Jo chased after fellers like they'd just been invented. Over the moon one minute, in tears the next. And then she had the gall to have a go at *her* because she happened to like one now and again. Enjoy a mature relationship with a mature man. What was wrong with that, for God's sake? Anyway, she knew what she was doing. She wasn't a silly little cow like Jo. And, having fully justified her feelings for Ashley Young, she started to think about him and continued to think about him until she drifted off into a deep sleep.

It was eleven o'clock the next day when Sister Rothwell told her that Ashley was to be discharged that afternoon. 'You'll organize him, won't you, Nurse?' she said with a leer that made Ruth suspect she probably read dirty books when she was not bullying her husband.

Ruth did not quite know whether to be happy or sad, the former because of the veiled suggestion that they might continue to see each other after he had left hospital (which he had never since enlarged upon), or the latter because he would no longer be on tap, as it were. Ashley put her mind at rest when she went to ask him if he wanted her to ring his wife and tell her to bring his clothes. He thanked her and then said, 'Where can I ring you?'

'Ring me?' She knew perfectly well what he meant, although she still felt uneasy.

'Yes, ring you. Here?'

'No, they don't like us taking personal calls.'

'Where, then?'

'Where I live. I share a flat.'

'Somewhere local?'

'Yes, Battersea.'

'When's the best time to phone you?'

'Well, evenings when I'm on days, like this week and next.'

'What's the number?'

She told him the number and he scribbled it down.

'I'll ring you Monday evening.'

'All right.'

Ruth was walking on air. Her own natural caution and Jo's warning occasionally brought her back to earth, but not for long. Her good sense told her that she might be playing with fire, but was it not better to be happy even spasmodically than to be permanently sick at heart as she had been at the beginning of the week? Sister Rothwell said tartly as she wheeled in the lunch trolley, 'Has Ashley not asked you to join him, Nurse, a sort of farewell meal together?'

'Not quite, Sister, not quite,' replied Ruth as mysteriously as she could manage, enjoying the opportunity to get one back at Sister Rothwell who looked quite put out, deflated in fact if that were possible for someone so solidly built.

Mrs Young arrived to collect her husband at half past two. He was helping Ruth to strip his bed when she walked into the ward looking perfect in a green smock and a white skirt. She nodded amicably to Ruth and handed her husband a suitcase containing some clothes. He took them into the bathroom to change and Mrs Young sat in a chair by the side of the bed, not talking, just watching Ruth work. For some reason Ruth began to feel uncomfortable, as if she were being closely scrutinized, sharply assessed; but when she glanced across at Mrs Young all that she saw was a very lovely woman with friendly eyes. Ashley returned, dressed in a blue double-breasted blazer and grey slacks, a combination which suited him even better than it does David Niven. Ruth wondered what she herself could possibly wear when he came to take her out. Her own wardrobe would hardly excite an Oxfam shop.

Ashley said, 'Well, thank you very much, Ruth, for looking after me. I couldn't have been in better hands. Really, I mean that. Thank you.' And he held out his hand which Ruth took: she found herself responding to its gentle but firm pressure which she was in no doubt was his private thank-you to her. And more than that, a promise.

'I'll just go and say goodbye to Sister, won't be a jiffy,' he said to his wife and with a last quick smile at Ruth he turned and walked out of the ward, calling his goodbyes to Mr Riley and young Michael and all the other patients as he went. Except old Mr Portman who was lying quite still with his eyes closed, no movement perceptible in his frail, overworked chest.

Mrs Young rose from her chair, moved to follow her husband, paused and turned to Ruth, who was collecting all the dirty linen from the floor. She said without a trace of rancour or even emotion, 'Oh Nurse, if you're expecting to see him again, I'm afraid you'll have a long wait. He'll have so many others to see first.' And she turned and walked quickly out of the ward, every male eye on her except Mr Portman's.

Ruth was left holding the mass of linen, feeling and looking rather ridiculous. Not for a second did she doubt that what Mrs Young had said was true. She would have believed Mrs Young if she had told her that the earth was flat. Mrs Young had that sort of authority. Ruth did not feel angry either, just defeated as she had on the station when she had caught the train back to London. Defeated not so much because she had been let down but because she had been proved wrong again. Was she always wrong about everything? It seemed so. And the corollary to that was that her mother must be right. All those wasted years being wrong . . .

'Nurse Fullman,' called Sister Rothwell from down the ward in what she fondly supposed was a whisper but which actually could probably have been heard in the street. Ruth put the linen down on the bed and joined Sister, who was drawing the curtains round Mr Portman's bed. She indicated the old man who looked as if he was carved in wax and said, 'I'm afraid the poor old soul's gone. Get Dr Carter, will you?' Ruth looked down at Mr Portman and for the first time since she was a very little girl, she started to cry.

St. Angela's Hospital

MERICI ROAD
LONDON S.W.11

HOSPITAL SCHOOL OF NURSING
CONFIDENTIAL REPORT

Surname Patel **Forenames** Sita

Date of birth 8/3/54 **Expected date of final examination** Spring 1976

Previous nursing or other relevant qualifications None

Confidential report

Sita, now in her third year of training, is a Ugandan Asian who has been in England for nearly four years. She and her family previously lived in Kampala, where her father ran a successful business until Amin's expulsion order. Sita has all the makings of a good nurse, but as yet she has not proved she can take decisions. Her hesitant manner does not instil confidence in the junior nurses, nor in the patients under her care. Apart from this, however, she is a good, conscientious nurse. Hopefully, by the end of the three-year training she will have gained sufficient experience to make an efficient, sound Staff Nurse.

Heather Windrup

Heather Windrup, Senior Nursing Tutor

SITA

'You've had another letter, haven't you?'

At first I didn't answer, busying myself with the inhalant. Hoping that she would get distracted and forget the question. We were in the ward clinical room, Ruth standing just behind the door, out of sight of the ward and Sister.

'Haven't you?' Her voice was insistent.

'Yes.' I tried to make it sound light, careless.

'What did they say this time?'

Outside a phone was ringing somewhere. A patient shuffled by, with weak, tottering steps. Ruth dropped her voice to a whisper.

'Sita, if you want me to mind my own business . . .'

'It is not that . . .'

'Well, what did they say?'

I sighed. 'They wanted to know if I had reached a decision.'

'And have you?'

The inhalants were ready. Taking one in each hand, I started to go, making for the ward.

'Have you?' Ruth's voice was sharp.

'Why do you press me like this?' I asked wearily. 'You know I have not.'

'Well, what are you going to *do*?' she asked earnestly. 'You can't avoid it for ever.'

I felt uneasy under her questioning. The heat from the inhalants was coming through and hurting my hands.

'I'll tell you what,' she went on in a milder tone, 'we'll talk about it at lunch-time. Sort something out.'

I smiled, relieved to drop the subject for a while. 'All right.'

'And Sita . . .' She put a hand on my arm. 'You've got to make up your mind soon. Because you know what'll happen if you don't. You'll get sucked in by it all. They'll write to you again and again until you do as they say just to avoid the sweat of making a decision.'

And with that she went, her shoes squeaking, off down the corridor.

I know the whole idea appalled Ruth. I suppose it did me in a way, the anglicized, integrated part of me anyway. Yet the notion of an arranged marriage shouldn't. I had grown up with the knowledge that it would happen, but the expulsion from Uganda, the settling in England, had pushed it out of all our minds. At least I thought it had, until I had received the letter from my parents about a month ago.

I told Ruth about it one lunch hour, about a week after the letter arrived. We were walking by the river and I suddenly told her. I don't know why. I suppose I felt the need to discuss it with someone and she happened to be there. At first she thought I was joking. I finally had to read her part of the letter before she believed me. Then she went quiet for a long time. We sat on a bench by the river. It was one of those grey, London sort of days, undecided whether to drizzle or be sunny. When she did speak, she did it without looking at me, her eyes on the water.

'What will you do?'

'I'm not certain.'

'Have you met him, this . . .?'

'Lachman,' I said. 'Lachman Desai. He is the son of the family my parents live with in Leicester. I met him there.'

'What's he like?' Her tone was curious.

'Like?' I asked.

'How old is he?'

'Thirty.'

'Did you get on with him?'

I had difficulty in even recalling Lachman's features, let alone my reaction to him. When I told Ruth that, she abruptly started to laugh.

'My God, it's primitive. Here you are, a nurse, living an independent life, and suddenly you get a letter from your parents asking you to chuck it all in to marry some bloke you've hardly met!'

I shifted around uneasily in my seat. The impulse that had initially prompted me to confide in Ruth had gone, leaving in its wake an embarrassed confusion. Ruth is one of those assured, confident sort of people, with a clear, incisive mind. Sitting next to her on that bench, I felt like a frail, indeterminate echo. My poor use of spoken English didn't help. It made everything I said sound formal and cold, all the feeling strangled out of it. I thought for a moment before speaking, trying to organize my thoughts.

'It is a question of custom, Ruth,' I said finally. 'It is the custom of my people for the parents to arrange the marriage of their daughters. The selection is careful . . .' I paused. She was looking at me now, expectantly. 'This Lachman,' I went on. 'We owe his family much. My father has known his parents for some time. When we first came from Uganda, they offered us their house. Made their home ours. We are in their debt.'

'So you're to be the sacrificial lamb!' Ruth said bitterly. 'A token of your parents' gratitude. You marry this bloke and honour is satisfied. The debt is paid.'

She looked across the river, her expression angry. 'I could understand it if you were still part of it all. Your parents' Hindu community and all that. But you're not. You've lived in London for over two years, found your own way . . . You can't just pretend those two years haven't happened.'

The bluntness of Ruth's words struck me more forcibly than I cared to admit. In her direct way, she had immediately seized upon the truth, and having done so, began to worry at it, like a dog with a bone.

'It's obvious you hate the whole idea,' she went on. 'If you didn't you'd never have told me about it.' She stopped, as the thought struck her. 'Why *did* you tell me about it?'

I shrugged. 'I wanted advice.'

'I'm not sure I can advise you, Sita. Or that I should even . . .' She hesitated fractionally. 'Supposing you refused, just wrote saying it was out of the question. What would they do?'

'Do?'

'Your parents,' said Ruth pointedly. 'Would they chuck you out, never speak to you again, or what . . . ?'

'It will be difficult to refuse them.' I thought of my parents, of my mother Saveeta, and her entreaties in the letter.

'Of course it'll be difficult,' Ruth said impatiently. 'Anyone can see that. But they'd get over it, wouldn't they?'

'I am not quite sure it is as simple as that,' I said slowly. 'To refuse them would mean . . .' I stopped, uncertain how to put it.

'Mean what?'

'It would mean rejecting everything. Not just them. But their whole way of life.' I paused and then added rather selfconsciously, 'My culture.'

'Hmm.'

We fell silent for a minute. Ruth was plucking at a splinter of wood in the bench, prising it loose with her thumb and forefinger.

'This has been brewing for some time, hasn't it?' she said at last. 'Not just this marriage thing. But the whole set-up. The way you never go out anywhere, to a pub or anything, because it might go against your background . . . And all those letters home, clinging to your parents.' She shot me a quick, surreptitious glance, assessing the effect of her words. 'I can't advise you, Sita. You've got to decide this one for yourself. If there is a break to be made, only you can do it.' And she stood up and started walking back up the path along the river.

That was four weeks ago. Shortly after, I was transferred to another ward, so I didn't see Ruth for some time, except to nod to in the canteen or sprinting down the corridor on some errand. I was relieved. Ruth, in my mind, had become part of the tangled nightmare of indecision.

During those weeks I received several more letters. At first Lachman had been mentioned obliquely, just one of the many scribbled details about their lives in Leicester. But now the references became more pointed – more difficult to ignore. Finally, on the morning that Ruth pinned me down in the clinical room, I had received this last letter.

Dear Daughter,
I have been so worried because you haven't written. You are not ill, I hope? We are all busy here, planning Diwali,* I can't believe it is only a few weeks away. It seems like only yesterday we were all together, celebrating it last year . . . I do hope you'll be able to come home for it, Sita. I know Lachman is especially anxious to see you. He talks about you so much . . . It will be so much better when you are living up here again. We miss you so much,

*Diwali = Hindu New Year, celebrated in October.

and when you don't write, we get so worried, Sita . . .

I must sign off because Mina is going to post this on her way to school. Write back soon, child. We will expect you for Diwali, unless we hear otherwise. Your father will want to know your decision by then, Sita. I know you will not disappoint him. The Desais send their love, as do I.

Your mother, Saveeta.

It was written on a scrap of lined paper. Mina, my little sister, had probably torn it out of her school exercise book. I suspected my mother had written it without my father's knowledge. As head of the family it was his duty to select my future husband, and I assumed that Mother, worried by my unusual silence, had hastily scribbled me the note, hoping to prompt me into a reply.

The morning seemed to drag by, my lunchtime appointment with Ruth hanging heavily over me. Sister asked me to prepare an old man for an operation. He was a frail, withered old man with puffy eyes and a sunken chest. As I was washing him, he kept asking me what day it was, and each time I told him he repeated it after me, in a bewildered, anxious voice.

'I thought it was Thursday,' he said. 'I was told it was Thursday.'

'That was yesterday.'

'Yesterday?' He stared at me vacantly.

'Today is Friday.' I glanced up at the clock at the end of the ward. Only half an hour until lunch.

'I was told it was Thursday.' He said it accusingly, as if he had been deliberately misinformed.

'Can you lift your arm, Mr Evans? So I can wash you?'

He obediently lifted one arm, holding it over his head like a child seeking attention from his teacher. As I washed him, my mind wandered back to the letter. 'Your father will want to know your decision by then, Sita. I know you will not disappoint him.' Then quite suddenly I knew what I had to do. It seems extraordinary, looking back on it, that the decision should come then, at that moment, out of nowhere. Perhaps it was because the old man I was washing seemed so helpless, so utterly unable to control either his thoughts or the events that happened to him. Next to his childlike dependence I seemed strong and vital. A sense of my own individuality hit me, perhaps for the first time. I remembered something my father had once said to me, years ago, in Uganda. 'There are two kinds of people, Sita. Those who make decisions, and those who have decisions made for them.' He had been referring to himself then. To his successful business that he had built up from nothing. Odd that his words should come back to me now, and be the inspiration that would set me against him.

I met Ruth in the canteen; she was already seated at a table waiting for me. When I told her about my decision she beamed at me, obviously relieved.

'When will you do it?' she asked. 'No point in putting it off now you've decided.'

'That depends on you.'

'On me?'

'I have been to see Sister,' I told her. 'She says I may go this afternoon. But there is need . . .' The words were getting jumbled around in my excitement.

'Steady on. Need for what?'

'My duty tomorrow,' I spoke more slowly. 'If I go away, someone must stand in for me tomorrow.'

'And you want me to?'

'I know it is your day off, Ruth . . .'

'Say no more.' She grinned at me.

'You are sure you do not mind?' I asked.

'Positive.' She paused. 'If you promise me one thing.'

'What?'

'That you won't get cold feet. Duck out of it at the last minute.'

'Why should I do that?'

She was silent for a moment. The tannoy shrieked a message over our heads. 'Medical Social Worker to Ward 14 please. Ward 14.'

'Why should I?' I said again.

'Deciding is one thing. Carrying it out is another.'

I looked at her. 'You think I cannot do it?'

'You said yourself it would be difficult,' she pointed out. 'I'm not trying to discourage you. I think you're doing the right thing. All I'm saying is . . .'

'You think I am not strong enough,' I said flatly. 'That is what you are saying.'

'Not at all!' She looked aggrieved that I should suggest such a thing. 'I'm simply saying that you made up your mind very quickly. I mean, a few hours ago you didn't have a clue what you were going to do. Now, suddenly, you've decided. You can hardly have thought it out in that time.'

'But . . .' I was bewildered. 'Is not that what you said I should do? Make a decision?'

'Sita!' She sounded exasperated. 'You mustn't worry about *me*. I'm not you. I think you should make a decision, I'm delighted you have. But it's not like you to suddenly do things, you're more . . .' She hesitated. 'Cautious. You always think before you act. Look before you leap. Now suddenly, about something so important, you make up your mind just like that!'

'Perhaps I have changed.'

'Perhaps you have.' She looked at me doubtfully, then brightened. 'Oh well. You've decided, that's the main thing. Who am I to question the whys and wherefores? When d'you leave?'

Two hours later I was on the train to Leicester. Watching the countryside float past the grimy window, I felt all my previous elation dissipating. I was drinking coffee from one of those plastic cups that hurt your hands, and thinking about what lay ahead. I had telephoned my mother at work to say I would be coming, and she had promised that someone would be at the station to meet me. I just hoped it wouldn't be my father. I wasn't ready to see him yet.

The conversation with Ruth had left me flat and dejected. I cursed myself for letting her pierce my newly acquired confidence so easily. Our friendship had been a curious one. We had little in common, either in our backgrounds or characters, yet I had always felt drawn to her. Perhaps because she had this blunt kind of assurance, a way of greeting life head on, defying it to harm her. During the two years I had been nursing I had come increasingly to depend on Ruth. It wasn't intentional, yet it had become the substance of our relationship. Sitting there, in that train, recollecting my many conversations with her, I suddenly had an odd sensation. As if the premise of our friendship was suddenly, and inexplicably, thrown into question. Then I realized what it was. All the things that I had assumed about Ruth, the confidence, the self-assurance, had been totally in my own mind. I recognized her for what she was – just an ordinary girl. Oh, she had determination, a bluntness of manner, but they didn't necessarily stem from an inner sense of certainty; probably from just the opposite. Underneath that confident mask she was probably as doubtful and insecure as I was . . . It was a strange sensation, looking at Ruth from this new viewpoint. Rather like when one first realizes that one's parents are simply frail, ordinary people, with weaknesses like everyone else. That they are capable of mistakes, and that when they 'kissed it better' they were merely cheating you, because they had no such power . . .

I began to wonder, with a sudden sinking feeling, if my inspired decision to reject my parents' wishes hadn't stemmed from some hidden desire to please Ruth, because it was what she wanted me to do. I tried to push the thought from my mind, but it kept returning, taunting me. I drank the last of the coffee, cold by now, and looked out of the window. I could see the carriage reflected in it. My suitcase up on the rack, the table littered with plastic cups and magazines. Then I felt an unexpected stab of panic. I couldn't see myself. I couldn't see my own reflection . . . The carriage all round me was there, perfectly mirrored in the grimy surface of the window. Yet I wasn't. After a second I realized why. The angle of my seat prevented me from being reflected in the window. My hands felt damp and clammy and I rubbed them on my coat, chiding myself for my stupidity. But just for a fleeting, unnerving moment, it had been as if I didn't exist . . .

The train was late pulling into Leicester, and I was horrified to see Lachman standing at the barrier waiting for me. He was rather an absurd sight, with his short, stocky figure standing slightly apart from the crowd, clutching a bunch of flowers. I felt an irrepressible urge to giggle as I trudged up the platform towards him. The tubby little figure waiting to greet me hardly coincided with the ogre I had built up in my mind. To my relief he didn't mention the marriage on the drive back to the house. He had an old van, which, as he told me proudly, he serviced and maintained himself. He rattled on about the difficulty of getting parts, the inaccuracy of his service manual and the exorbitant price of petrol, hardly drawing breath between each sentence. As he talked I shot him unobtrusive, sidelong glances. The most distinctive thing about him was his hands. Childlike hands, with short plump fingers. I observed, with a kind of detached curiosity, that he had dirt under his fingernails. His eye caught mine for a moment, and he immediately looked away, embarrassed. He's shy, I thought. Shy and nervous. I felt a sudden twinge of compassion for him. It's easy to feel compassion when you are not the victim, and that's how Lachman struck me at that moment. The victim of my decision. I had a sudden urge to confide in him. To tell him that I couldn't possibly marry him, but just as I built up courage to say it, the van pulled up outside the house. We were there.

The first person to greet me was my grandmother. She stood on the steps, her arms outstretched, a small, frail figure in a red sari. As I walked towards her, she ran forward, clasping me in her arms, muttering endearments in Gujarati.* Then my mother came out, almost shyly, to meet me. She scrutinized my face carefully, holding my hand in hers, her dark eyes probing mine.

'Sita,' she said, 'I've missed you, child.' She folded me into her arms, gave me the briefest of hugs and then stood aside. My father was standing in the doorway, beaming at me.

'Such a surprise,' he said. 'And we have you for a whole weekend, I hear?'

'Until Sunday,' I replied.

He glanced over my head at Lachman, who was waiting awkwardly behind me with my suitcase. I turned in time to see a quick glance of complicity pass between them. My mother touched my arm.

'The Desais are waiting to see you, Sita. And Mina is so excited. She has talked of nothing else ever since she came home from school.'

* Gujarati is Sita's native tongue.

We trooped inside, my grandmother still clinging on to me. She had grown older since my last visit home, three months before. Her steps were weak, and her hands shook as she reached out to support herself. She reminded me of my patients, and I realized, with a pang of guilt, that she would be dead soon and that I was cheating her out of the ritual of a family marriage.

As we entered the small front room of the house, I found myself shuddering involuntarily. I remembered the feeling of claustrophobia that this house always gave me. It had been that feeling that had prompted me into leaving two years ago, when I grabbed at the opportunity to go to London to train as a nurse.

The house was one of those small, Victorian terrace ones. Altogether seven of them lived in it: Lachman and his parents, and my own family, comprising my grandmother, Father, Mother and little sister Mina, who was now twelve years old. I imagined little had been done to the house since the Desais had moved into it some eight years before. The wallpaper was faded, of the floral kind that runs in vertical patterns and stops just below the picture railing. The ceilings, though high, were covered with polystyrene tiles which had yellowed with age. Only the furniture seemed new. Brightly coloured, nylon-covered armchairs cluttered the floor and a large colour television set stood in one corner, blinking vacantly into the room.

The Desais themselves were considerably older than my parents. Mohan Desai, Lachman's father, was about sixty, and his wife Santa about two years younger. Mohan, like Lachman, was a small man, but unlike Lachman, he was a dominating sort of person with a deep, resonant voice. He seemed to fill the room, despite his diminutive stature, pushing even my father into insignificance. He was a quality inspector in a local cloth factory, and his job and experience of the English way of life had given him a kind of anglicized sophistication that my family had yet to acquire. It had been Mohan who had written to my father in Uganda, offering us their home, and it had been he who had finally found my father a job in his factory. The obligation we all felt towards this squat, powerful little man is hard to put into words. Yet at the same time, I have occasionally sensed a kind of unspoken resentment towards him in my parents' attitude. It's the kind of resentment that one feels about any landlord, I suppose. No matter how kind, how decent they are, how reasonable the rent is, one resents them simply because they *are* landlords. Not that Mohan ever acted like one, but the fact that it was his house my family lived in, his beds they slept in, added a strain on their relationship. In Uganda my parents had known considerable wealth. My father had owned a chain of supermarkets in the city centre, and we had lived in a large, luxurious house on the outskirts of Kampala. Suddenly, almost overnight, they had lost it all. I often marvelled at the way my parents had accepted the abruptness of that transition. From the quiet wealth of that house in Kampala, nestling in the valley, to the grey urbanness of this somewhat bleak little house in Leicester.

Mohan Desai rose to greet me, using an incongruous combination of Gujarati and English. He grasped my hand firmly in his, placing his other hand over mine, squeezing it as he spoke.

'Ah, Sita,' he smiled and a gold tooth glinted at me. 'Welcome home.'

The word 'home' jarred, but I smiled back at him, with the same perfunctory smile that I used on the ward.

'It's nice to be here.'

'Lachman was on time, I hope?'

'Waiting at the barrier.'

'Good, good.' He released my hand. 'You are tired I expect, from the journey?'

'A little, I suppose.'

Santa Desai, standing a little behind her husband, coughed slightly. He stood aside, and she beamed at me, clasping my arms. She had an angular, almost jagged face, and wore a pale turquoise sari elegantly swathed over her shoulders and her greying hair. She was a distinguished-looking woman, who ran her home with quiet, rigid efficiency.

'Well, Sita,' she said in her even voice. 'Your room is all ready for you, just as it always is. You want to go up and wash before we eat?'

I nodded, and, placing her hand under my arm, she led me out of the room, whilst my parents called out a ragged chorus of endearments after me. We climbed the stairs to the small room at the back of the house which I was to share with Mina. The room was neat, with two beds placed side by side, separated by a small bed-table in the middle. Mina lay on one of the beds, a pile of schoolbooks in front of her. As we entered she looked up expectantly, her face combining pleasure at seeing me with a childish sort of shyness, which made her look rather coquettish, the way children often do when they first encounter an adult.

'Hello, Mina,' I said. 'What's that you're doing?'

'Schoolwork,' she said with a grimace.

'What subject?'

'Chemistry. We've an exam tomorrow.'

Santa reached out and ruffled her hair. 'Our Mina is doing well at school. She came fourth in her class last term, didn't you?'

Mina nodded, her eyes taking in my London-bought sweater and skirt. I noted the maternal tone in Santa's voice, similar to the one she used with me. Having no daughters of her own, she had welcomed us into her house particularly warmly, and I could see that Mina identified with her as closely as she did with our own mother.

We heard footsteps on the stairs and my father entered with my suitcase. He and Santa then withdrew, shutting the door behind them. Mina, suddenly finding herself alone with me, looked down at her schoolbooks. I sat down on the bed opposite her. Our window overlooked the backs of other houses, identical to this one, and rooftops stretched away endlessly into the evening light. They had turned up the television downstairs and the jangle of an advertisement echoed vaguely through the house. I could hear the deep voices of Mohan Desai and my father in conversation and crockery rattling in the kitchen as the preparations for the evening meal got under way. I lay back on the bed, looking at the ceiling. I would have to say something soon. There was an air of expectancy in the house, and that look I had caught between Lachman and my father . . . I decided that I would talk to my mother about it, after supper, while we were washing up. Santa always joined the men in the front room whilst Mother did the dishes. That would be my opportunity.

'Sita?' Mina was standing by the bed, looking down at me.

I sat up and smiled at her. 'What is it?'

'I've made you something.' She pulled out a parcel from behind her back. 'I did it in dressmaking. Mother said you'd be needing lots, so I thought I'd make you one.'

I took the parcel from her and unwrapped it. It was a sari, crimson with pale blue flowers embroidered on it in small crests around the border.

'D'you like it?'

'It's lovely.' I rubbed my fingers over the flowers. 'Really lovely, Mina.'

'I'll make you another if you want. It didn't take long.'

'You ought to make something for yourself.'

'I don't need one.' She flung herself on her bed, crushing her schoolbooks. 'Besides,' she added with childlike tactlessness, 'Mother told me to make it.'

'It's very nice.' I stood up and started to pull off my sweater.

'What are you doing?'

I waited until my head was free of the sweater and said, 'I'm going to put it on, of course.'

'Now?'

'Why not?'

'But . . .' Mina was staring at me, her large, rather mournful dark eyes fixed anxiously on mine.

'But what? Don't you want me to wear it?'

'Yes, but . . .'

'Well, then.' I picked it up and started to twine it round myself, watching my reflection in the mirror. I hadn't worn a sari for some weeks, and as I hung it over my shoulders I suddenly took on the appearance of my mother and Santa, my skin seemed to grow darker and my face to change as I draped the cloth around my head. I looked at myself for a minute, observing the transition with mixed feelings. Mina was staring at me, with a disturbed look on her face.

'Don't you like it?' I asked her.

'It looks lovely. But . . .' She picked up an end and felt it in her hand. 'You were supposed to keep it. It was for your trousseau.'

I stared at her. 'For my trousseau?'

'Santa's made you some as well,' said Mina. She stood up and started to adjust the sari around me, checking my reflection in the mirror. 'It took me ages to do that embroidery. It's all done by hand.'

My reflection stared blandly back at me, the reference to my trousseau still ringing in my ears. It is the custom of our people for the bride to have a wardrobe full of saris for her wedding, and I was suddenly apprehensive, realizing how completely my parents and the Desais assumed this marriage was going to take place. Mina started to collect up her schoolbooks, and I watched her carefully, wondering how much I could confide in her.

'Have they said anything to you, Mina?' I said at last. 'Mother or Father or anyone?'

'Said anything about what?'

'Lachman. The wedding.'

She paused, the books balanced on her arm. 'Not really. They're all very excited about it though. Why?'

'No reason.' I looked down at the sari; the fading light was catching the flowers, making them three-dimensional and alive. 'I'd better take this off, then.'

'Yes. And I'd better help with the supper. See you in a minute.' She clattered off downstairs and I took one last look at myself. I'd talk to my mother as soon as supper was over. Definitely.

But supper came and went, and still I had said nothing. Santa wouldn't hear of my helping in the kitchen on my first evening home, so after supper I sat in the front room with Lachman, Mohan and my father. They had cleared the table and were all seated around it, playing Scrabble. Mohan declared it was the best possible way to learn English, and he and my father challenged Lachman and Mina to a game. I turned on the television and sat on the sofa in front of it, listening to their laughter and wondering when and how I was going to bring up the subject of Lachman. After a few moments my mother came and sat next to me. There was an American crime film on television. The sound was turned down low, so as not to disturb the Scrabble game, but mother and I sat and watched the pictures. A man was being chased through some streets by another man, and somewhere high up on a building a sniper sat with a rifle, waiting to shoot someone. My mother sat silently next to me, her eyes on the television. Finally she spoke very softly, so that the others wouldn't hear.

'I have been so worried, Sita.'

I glanced at her. The image of the television flickered in her eyes.

'Worried? Why?'

'Because you didn't write.'

I looked back at the television. The man being chased had run down a subway.

'I had to think things out,' I said. 'I didn't mean to worry you. It's just . . .' I hesitated, my courage failing.

'I was afraid you were ill,' my mother continued in a low voice. 'Or that something had happened. So much happens in London. I thought, perhaps she has met some boy, that is why we do not hear from her. There was a programme on about Asian girls who live away from home. Many had white boyfriends, but didn't dare to tell their parents. I thought . . .' she shot me a quick, apologetic look. 'Maybe you had met someone and you were frightened of telling us.'

The man in the film was trapped down the subway. He kept running up blind tunnels and having to double back on himself. Behind him the other man was closing in. He had a knife stuck in his belt under his jacket.

'Is there a boy, Sita?' my mother asked softly.

'No one special, Mother. I have been out to a party with one boy . . . But there is no one special.'

'I'm glad.' She looked relieved. Behind us the Scrabble game was in full swing. Mohan was laughing hilariously, calling out the score in triumph. He was obviously winning.

'Lachman is such a good man, Sita. And he needs you.' My mother glanced over her shoulder at him, lowering her voice. 'He has bought this shop. A corner shop in Clifton Street. He put the deposit down last week. He is going to give up his job in the factory and run the shop, so you'll be able to help him . . . His English is good, but he is so shy, Sita. He needs someone like you, used to working with people, to help. You'll live here of course, with Mohan and Santa. Father and I should be moving out shortly, we have seen a flat we think we can get. You'll be able to have our room. It'll need doing up of course . . .'

I listened in silence, watching the television. The sniper, it turned out, was waiting for the man with the knife. As he was climbing the steps from the subway the sniper shot him in the back. I spoke quietly, cutting through my mother's voice, my eyes fixed on the television, watching the man writhe on the pavement whilst a small crowd gathered round him.

'I cannot marry Lachman, Mother.'

'I bought you a book of wallpaper patterns,' my mother went on. 'The room is so dark at the moment. I've spoken to the Desais and they don't mind you decorating it.'

For a moment I wondered if I'd actually spoken, if I'd actually managed to form the words. Then my mother broke off and stared at me.

'I'm sorry, Mother,' I said. 'But I cannot marry him.'

'Sita!' She breathed in sharply. 'What is this you are saying?'

'I've thought about it ever since you wrote to me.' A sudden gust of laughter from the Scrabble table interrupted me. Mohan called out.

'Sita! This boy of mine will do you credit. He's won the first round.'

'Oh?' I smiled over the back of the sofa, then turned back to my mother.

'I am sorry, Mother,' I said again. 'I had to tell you.'

'Why are you doing this to us?' she asked dully.

'I'm not doing it to hurt you,' I replied. 'I don't want to marry him, that's all.'

The film on television was ending. Bright yellow letters jostled with each other on the screen. My mother watched them through unseeing eyes, her fingers nervously plucking at her sari.

'You need time to think,' she whispered. 'You'll realize what it is that you are doing when you have thought about it.'

'I have thought about it, Mother,' I replied wearily. 'I've thought about nothing else for weeks.'

She started to rock back and forth, her eyes fixed on the television screen. I reached out and squeezed one of her hands.

'I really am sorry,' I said helplessly.

'Sorry!' She barked the word out. 'Don't tell me you're sorry.

Tell Lachman. Tell your father . . .' She broke off. My hand holding hers suddenly felt moist and I saw with horror that she was crying. Silent tears trickled down her chin and then leapt with a splash onto our hands, clasped together on her lap. Behind us the murmur of conversation at the Scrabble table continued. I glanced over my shoulder, afraid that they would hear my mother's quiet whimpering.

'Everything was ready,' she said in a shocked, faint voice. 'It was all planned. The Desais . . .' She stopped, shooting an apprehensive glance at Mohan. 'Someone will have to tell them.'

'I will.'

She turned to look at me, her face suddenly hard. 'Do it now, then. If you must. Do it now.' And she stood up and left the room. The party at the Scrabble table hardly seemed to notice her departure. They were struggling over some word, looking in a dictionary to check its meaning. For a few moments I continued watching the silent television. There was a comedy show on, and a man was demonstrating how to put up an umbrella, except that it was broken, and kept collapsing every time he hoisted it up. I found myself smiling, in spite of my tension. Then abruptly, before my courage could fail me again, I stood up and switched off the television and turned to face them. The nervousness and indecision of the last weeks had gone, and all I felt now was a kind of dull resignation. My father noticed me first.

'Come and join us, Sita!' he called out cheerfully. 'Mina is hopeless. She spells everything wrong.'

I cleared my throat. 'I have something to say.'

I surprised myself with the calm way I delivered the words, almost as if I were announcing I'd make a cup of tea.

A sudden hush fell over the group at the table. Mohan twisted round in his seat to look at me.

'It concerns Lachman,' I said in the same calm voice.

Lachman looked startled at the sound of his name. I forced myself to look directly at him, locking his eyes with mine.

'I'm sorry,' I said quickly, 'I can't marry you. That's why I came home this weekend, to tell you. I wanted to tell you on the way from the station, but I couldn't find the words . . .'

He stared calmly at me, his eyes devoid of expression. I couldn't meet that blank, vacant look. I shifted my eyes away.

'I'm sorry,' I said yet again. I didn't know what else to say.

Lachman looked down at a Scrabble square in his hand. It lay in his palm and for a moment his hand closed round it, gripping it tightly, then, very carefully, he placed it on the table. He stood up, scraping his chair back and, without looking at me or anyone else, he walked out of the room.

There was a long silence, interrupted by my father's sharp intake of breath.

'Mina. Go upstairs.'

'But Father . . .'

'Upstairs!' He practically shouted it.

Mina, with visible reluctance, left the room. Mohan also rose, but my father stopped him.

'You stay, Mohan.'

'This is between you and her,' Mohan said. His normally jovial face looked suddenly old.

'This is between us all,' said my father. 'It is your son she is rejecting.'

Mohan slumped back into his chair. Mechanically he started rearranging the Scrabble pieces on the board. My father stood up and closed the door. He leant against it for a minute, his eyes on my face.

'Well,' he said at last. 'Are we to have an explanation?'

'I can't marry him,' I said simply.

'You reject my choice?'

'I reject . . .' I hesitated. 'I reject your right to choose my husband for me.'

'You realize what you are saying, Sita?' His face looked oddly contorted, his mouth twisted slightly to one side.

'I want to choose my own husband. Is that so unreasonable?'

'You have met some boy in London. Someone you prefer?'

'No, Father. I simply want to decide things for myself. I'm not ready to marry yet . . .'

Mohan shifted uneasily in his seat.

'Shanti, I really think . . .'

'And for that you humiliate your mother and me?' said Father, ignoring Mohan. 'That is what your two years in London have taught you, is it? To disregard the wishes of your parents and humiliate them?'

'Father, please . . .'

'Lachman is a good man,' he went on in a hard voice. 'You think I would have chosen him otherwise?'

'I'm sure he is,' I replied, glancing at Mohan, who was awkwardly fiddling with the Scrabble pieces. 'That is not the point, though. I just don't want to marry yet. Not Lachman or anyone.'

Mohan abruptly stood up. 'I don't want to hear this, Shanti,' he said, avoiding looking at me, 'I will wait upstairs until you have finished.'

He crossed to the door and my father stood aside, letting him pass. It was a while before either of us spoke. It was finally my father who broke the silence. His voice had lost some of its anger. It sounded bewildered and hurt.

'Why are you doing this, Sita? You have always been guided by me. Have I ever suggested you do a bad thing? It was I who encouraged you to do your nursing – you were frightened at first, remember? You didn't want to go. But I was right. You have made a good nurse. We're proud of you. And I am right in this. Trust me again, Sita. You will see I am right.'

He was practically pleading with me. It embarrassed me to see him do it, and I crossed to the table, putting the Scrabble squares away with my back to him, so that I wouldn't have to see it.

'Why do you want me to give up nursing, then,' I asked, 'if you're so proud of me?'

'Because Lachman will have the shop. You won't need to nurse any more.'

'But I want to!'

'You have proved you can do it,' said my father, genuinely puzzled. 'Why must you continue?'

'Because I haven't even finished my training yet!' I turned to face him. 'Besides, I'm not a particularly good nurse, Father.' He was about to interrupt me, but I carried on before he could. 'Oh, I know you think I am. Because I am your daughter, and you're naturally proud of me. But I'm not. On the ward . . . If I have to take a decision, you know what happens? I go to pieces. I refer it to Sister, or whoever I can. Anything, so that I can avoid taking the decision myself. Because it's not in my background to take decisions, Everything is decided for me, right down to the choice of my own husband.'

'But that is the way it should be.'

'For you perhaps. For your generation. It never really mattered when we were in Kampala, when I stayed at home all day helping in the house. But now everything's changed. And I have to change with it.'

He was still staring at me, with that puzzled expression on his face. I wondered how much of what I was saying was making any sense to him.

'If you make me marry Lachman now, I'll always know it was my escape route. That I did it because I couldn't cope out there.' I gestured vaguely towards the window. 'And I'd resent him because of it, Father. And you.'

'If we were to ask Lachman,' said Father carefully, 'I'm sure he would let you continue nursing. You could work in the local hospital perhaps . . .'

'But it's not just the nursing, is it?' I replied. 'It's us, taking refuge in our customs because it makes us feel secure. That's why it would be the easy way out, me marrying Lachman. I'd be doing it for all the wrong reasons.'

My father crossed the room to an armchair and sat down. He stared at the blank screen of the television set for a minute, then said in a dull voice, 'All the wrong reasons, you say. When it has always been our custom for the father to arrange the marriage of his daughter? And now, suddenly, you know better.'

'I hardly know the man, Father!'

'You know enough.' He looked across at me. 'You know his family. You know he works hard. That he is honest, that his prospects are good . . . Few English girls know so much about their future husbands.'

'But I don't know *him*! We've only exchanged a few words with each other!'

'But *I* know him,' my father suddenly exclaimed. 'I have lived with that boy, Sita, for over two years. I know all there is to know about him. You could not wish for a better man.'

'I'm sure he's very nice, Father. I just don't want to marry him, that's all.'

'And that is what I am to tell Mohan, is it? That his son isn't good enough for you?'

'I simply want to choose my husband,' I replied wearily. 'In my own time. In my own way.'

'So you do not trust my choice?'

'Just why is it so important to you?' I asked with a sudden spark of anger. 'Because it's Mohan's son I'm rejecting, and because you owe Mohan?'

'That has nothing to do with it,' my father said swiftly. 'I have told you my reasons for choosing Lachman.'

'And I'm sure you believe them,' I said, marvelling at my courage to speak to my father like this. 'But you and Mother don't realize ... The Desais have become like an obsession to you both. I know they've done a lot for us. Given us a home, found you your job ... But in every letter you wrote, you talked of nothing else. Hardly any mention of Mina or my grandmother. It was always the Desais, until I'm sick of hearing their name. And now you want me —' I remembered Ruth's words by the river on that grey day in London – 'to be the sacrificial lamb. To live in this house after you've gone, as a token of your gratitude. Well, I won't do it, Father. It's my life we're talking about. My career you want me to give up, and I simply will not do it!' My father didn't speak for a full minute. He sat, a rigid, proud figure in his chair, looking at me from across the room.

'And that is your last word?' he said eventually in a tightly controlled voice.

'Yes.'

'Then I suggest you leave first thing in the morning.' He got up and walked to the door. 'In the meantime, I would be grateful if you didn't discuss this with Mina, I don't want her ...' He hesitated and for a moment I thought he was going to say 'corrupted'. But 'disturbed' is what he finally said, before he walked out of the room.

For a moment I stood perfectly still, listening to his footsteps climbing the stairs. A door closed somewhere, and the house fell suddenly silent. The Scrabble squares were strewn across the table and I started idly to collect them together. Then I saw the dictionary. It was an old, dog-eared one, its cover half-curled back on itself. It was lying flat on the table and I picked it up to see if there was another Scrabble square underneath it. As I did so I happened to glance at the open page. It was open at the letter C, and I read this definition.

compromise: Meeting half way; coming to terms by giving up part of claim; middle course.

It's extraordinary, recollecting these events, that after so many weeks of tortured indecision my actions should be determined in such an apparently arbitrary way. By a book that happened to be open at a particular page. At that moment however, the thought of compromise appalled me. I shut the dictionary and tossed it into an armchair, as though trying to rid myself of its temptation.

Later that night something else happened. I was in bed, trying to sleep. Downstairs I could hear a dull murmur of voices, which I took to be my parents and the Desais discussing my decision. But then I heard a different, more regular sound, like a patient struggling for breath. Just for a second I thought it was Mina, lying asleep in the bed next to me, but it was too muffled and indistinct to be her. I got up and opened the door. It was coming from upstairs. I thought they were all downstairs but there was definitely someone upstairs. I paused for a moment in the hall, trying to discern where the noise was coming from. Then suddenly I recognized what it was. I had heard it on the ward several times. It was the sound of a man crying. Cautiously I pushed open the door of the bedroom next to mine. At first I thought it was my father lying there, prostrate on the bed, head cupped in hand, his body distorted by those dreadful, racking sobs. But it wasn't. It was Lachman. He didn't see me standing by the door, and I felt like an eavesdropper. He was lying face down, his back to me, and he was thumping the pillow with a clenched hand, rather like an angry, spoilt child. I must have stood there a full minute, my hand on the doorknob, watching him, before I finally slid out, carefully shutting the door behind me. I stood in the hall, listening to those muffled sobs. It seemed incredible. I was amazed that I was capable of arousing such feeling in anyone. Until that moment, even to myself, I had seemed to lack any kind of presence, like a vague echo that bounced off other people, but left no mark or impression on anyone. And yet, without knowing it, I had left an impression on Lachman. And he was in the next room, crying over me. And then I knew what I had to do. It wasn't as it had been in the ward, when I was washing Mr Evans and I'd suddenly been inspired with my decision to reject my father's wishes. This was different. Quieter, yet more certain. More concrete. I found myself remembering the words from the dictionary, 'Coming to terms by giving up part of claim; middle course.' And with those words in mind, I started the long climb downstairs.

The compromise was simple. I went over it on the train speeding back to London the next day, viewing it from all angles, like a sample of cloth, defying it to weaken under my scrutiny. We had decided, Mohan, my father and I, that the marriage should be postponed until I had finished training. During that year I would write to Lachman, and when I went home I would see him. If there was to be a relationship, I would give it the opportunity to flourish. However, if at the end of that time, I still felt reluctant, I would be released from the arrangement . . . We had solemnly worked it out, the three of us, like a contract, sitting round the table in that front room in the early hours of the morning. At first my father wouldn't listen, declaring it was degrading for the Desais to be expected to bargain over their son. But Mohan had been surprisingly reasonable. Perhaps his greater experience of England had made him more tolerant, I don't know. But he listened carefully to my proposition and finally it was he who persuaded my father into acquiescence.

I arrived back at the hospital at about half past nine. I was going straight to my room in the nurses' home, when some compulsion prompted me to go into the canteen. As soon as I entered, I knew why it was. Ruth was there. She had obviously just come off duty and she looked tired and fed up. Her hair was trailing limply down under her cap and she was reading an evening paper, sipping absentmindedly at a cup of tea.

I sat down opposite her, but it was a minute before she looked up. She beamed at me, with a smile of recognition.

'Sita! I didn't expect you back until tomorrow.'

'I decided to come back today. How was it, on the ward?'

'Oh, not too bad.' She pushed the paper to one side. 'Sister was on most of the time, so I wasn't in charge, thank God.' She paused, looking at me expectantly. 'What happened, then?'

'Happened?'

'At home. Did you tell them?'

'Yes. I told them,' I replied carefully.

'What did they do?'

I looked down at her tea. 'Have you finished?'

'Yeah.' She pushed the cup over. 'Help yourself. Did they threaten to chuck you out of house and home, or what?'

'At first, yes.'

'At first?' said Ruth curiously. 'Oh. They climbed down, did they? When they saw you meant it?'

'Climbed down?' I hadn't heard that expression before.

'Gave in. Compromised.'

That word again. 'No,' I said. 'It was I who compromised.'

'You!'

'That is right.'

'You mean . . .' She was staring at me disbelievingly. 'You're going through with it? You're going to marry him?'

'I did not say that.'

'Just what are you saying then?'

As I started to tell her, I thought, she's not going to understand. And suddenly, I became aware that I didn't care. I no longer cared what Ruth thought. It was a new, unfamiliar feeling and it took me a while to recognize it. As I expected, she expressed wholehearted contempt for the compromise and I realized, with a pang of regret, that this girl had never compromised on anything. Because she was that sort of person. One of the careless breed, who treat life as a battle to be fought and won. It would be the Ruths who would change things, who would make dramatic gestures and get the credit for them. Whilst I . . . I smiled, suddenly content for the first time in weeks. I would satisfy myself with the minor victories in life. With a compromise.

St. Angela's Hospital

MERICI ROAD
LONDON S.W. 11

HOSPITAL SCHOOL OF NURSING
CONFIDENTIAL REPORT

Surname Longhurst **Forenames** Josephine Mary Helen

Date of birth 27/2/56 **Expected date of final examination** Autumn 1976

Previous nursing or other relevant qualifications None

Confidential report

Josephine Longhurst is now in her second year of training. Her ward reports have, on the whole, been favourable. Nurse Longhurst does, however, have a tendency to put her emotions before nursing. She is, despite this, a resourceful, caring girl, with a sense of humour. If she can learn to distance herself from the problems of the patients, she should be a first-class nurse.

Heather Windrup

Heather Windrup, Senior Nursing Tutor

JO arrived for the night shift in rather a tizzy. She had had a row with Raoul – not serious and her own fault really. She was out of sorts as she always was when doing a stint on nights and the sight of Raoul grinning at another girl across the pub had been enough to give her the sulks and finally to goad the poor lad into a dramatic Gallic exit leaving her fuming into her orange juice. One blessing was that Night Sister on Female Medical was Betty Framley, who was very competent and also tended to trust her nurses more than most. She would be missing for long periods, suddenly reappearing just when she was required to deal with a crisis or to dispense advice. Jo thought she must have a feller in the boilerhouse and another theory was that she did a second job as a taxi driver. Sister rattled through the reports, which seemed to indicate a fairly quiet night: Jo herself rattled through the washing-up and tidying the kitchen and the sluice room because speed suited her temper. She helped with the drug round and dished out sleeping pills to those requiring them, which was virtually everybody, for sleep does not always come easily to those in hospital. By half past ten the ward had lapsed into as near a state of tranquillity as it ever did. It was never completely still: there was always the sound of people breathing, snoring, sighing, mumbling, even groaning; of beds creaking, muffled footsteps, and echoes from other parts of the hospital. It was an imperfect peace, but it was welcome.

Just after midnight Jo was mooning at Sister's desk after writing up her own reports and finishing off odds and ends of her other paperwork, such as drug charts and fluid charts. 'Mooning' can perhaps best be described as not quite daydreaming and not quite a brown study, more a sort of limbo of body and mind in which nothing much happens and which can be very pleasant. Mooning was a change for Jo, who was a busy little body normally. The phone rang to bring her back to the boil. It was Muriel, the operator, warning her that she was due for a visitor, and sure enough within ten seconds she heard a strangled whisper from just outside the door. 'Nurse, Nurse, help me, Nurse, I think I'm dying!' croaked somebody as if in extremis.

'Come in, Chris,' said Jo, without even looking up from the desk. On cue Chris Jackson poked his head round the door and said, 'How did you know it was me?'

'You're not the only one who has narks,' said Jo, smiling at him because she was pleased to see him.

'I'll have to have a word with Muriel,' said Chris, as he entered the office and parked his spare six-foot frame in a chair, raising one long leg and balancing the heel of his very shiny shoe on the edge of the desk.

'Comfortable enough?' she asked sarcastically.

'Very,' he said, not in the least offended.

Chris Jackson was a policeman, PC 40 actually, and St Angela's was on his calling list, which meant it was one of the score or so places in the area where he liked to drop in for a cuppa when his job allowed, which was not infrequently. He was in his mid-twenties, unmarried, intelligent, with an interesting rather than a handsome face because his nose was too big for one thing and his eyebrows too bushy. His best feature was a mouth which always seemed to be on the point of telling a joke. His pale-blue eyes tended to twinkle, too, especially when he was chatting up women, which he did even oftener than he drank free tea.

He said, solemnly for him, 'Had a report there's a prowler knocking about, so I thought I'd check here.'

'Isn't it time you found another excuse?' replied Jo.

'Eh?'

'Every time you come you say you're after a prowler.'

'I am.'

'There must be a lot of prowlers about.'

'There are. It's been a very good year for prowlers.'

'I don't believe a word you say about anything. And I'm not brewing up for at least another hour.'

'Not even if you had a snack to go with it?'

'Like what?' said Jo, suddenly interested.

'Like this.' He took a small parcel out of his tunic pocket and unwrapped the greaseproof paper to reveal two small but succulent steaks.

'Where did you get those?' asked Jo. 'Cor, aren't you the cadger.'

'They were given to me by a grateful member of the public

who I happened to render a service to tonight,' said Chris, adopting a PC Plodd accent. 'To whit, Frank Morris, the butcher down Frederick Road, who inadvertently forgot to lock his shop up and when I, being a conscientious bobby, discovered the fact and subsequently informed him, he was so grateful he thrust these two steaks into my hand and refused my efforts to return them, insisting he would be very upset if I did so. So not wishing to upset the said grateful member of the public, knowing full well the importance of maintaining good relations with the public, I had no alternative but to accept them with thanks.'

'Like you did the fish last week. Do you ever pay for anything?'

'Can I help it if I'm a good copper and the public are always feeling grateful to me, as well they should?' grinned Chris, innocent and impish at one and the same time. He could charm the birds out of the trees, never mind steaks out of butchers.

'You're a rogue, Chris Jackson,' said Jo, rising and picking up the steaks. 'I'll go and put them under the grill. I've not had a bite since breakfast as it happens. How would you like yours?'

'Just cooked,' said Chris following her into the kitchen across the corridor. 'You don't reckon I've found a way to your heart, do you? If I dropped the odd steak in now and again . . .'

'No, just to my stomach,' said Jo, enjoying the banter and matching him at it. It was a change, too, to talk to somebody articulate because Raoul's English was not all that good and a conversation with him could be a strain. Mind you, he had other gifts, though!

She switched on the cooker, put the steaks on the grill pan and put it under the grill. 'They look good enough to eat raw,' she said.

'Who's Night Sister?' asked Chris.

'Framley.'

'So I'm OK for an hour or two then.'

'Just as long as it takes you to eat.'

'Who's the new bloke, then?' asked Chris, changing the subject.

'What new bloke?'

'Ah come on, I'm the eye what never sleeps. This new bloke with the Peugeot with the French numberplates.'

'He must be a Frenchman.'

'Never,' said Chris. 'Well come on, who is he?'

'Wouldn't you like to know?' grinned Jo who, for all her natural effusiveness, could be very uncommunicative if she chose to be. The steak was cooking now and the aroma began to fill the kitchen. 'Hey, I hope Sister doesn't get a whiff of this,' said Jo, suddenly worried, but not very.

'That could be Framley in the car,' said Chris.

'What car?'

'Car parked just down the road with its windows all steamed up and somebody breathing very heavy in the back seat.'

'You know who that will be – Julie Woods and her latest.'

'Bit of all right Julie, isn't she?'

'If you like nymphos.'

'I do,' said Chris, his eyes shining and the message clear, but Jo wrinkled her nose at him and concentrated on the steak. The phone rang and she said, 'Watch these, don't let them burn.' She crossed back into the office and answered the phone. It was Muriel for Chris: 'Tell him he's got a visitor now, his Inspector.'

Oh dear, thought Jo, knowing full well that Chris's visits were meant to be clandestine, at least so far as some of his superiors were concerned. The better ones knew very well what went on, especially at night, but as long as the officers were instantly available via their personal radios, they turned a blind eye to their dropping in at St Angela's or Pitman's Bakery or the railway station for the odd ten minutes. It was only pubs and the beds of accommodating lady friends that were strictly forbidden.

Jo hurried back to the kitchen to warn Chris. 'Trouble,' she said, 'your Inspector's after you. He's here, in the building.'

'Hell,' said Chris, apparently alarmed – or as alarmed as he was ever likely to be about anything, for he was not a man who panicked easily. He had total faith in his ability to extricate himself from even the most unholy mess, a faith which he had already put to the test many times.

'It's Bonzo,' he said.

'Who?' asked Jo.

'Bonzo. Inspector Townsend to you. We call him Bonzo because when he's out with his wife, he always walks about half a step behind her just like a dog on a lead. She's bigger than he is, too. I'd better get lost. He's been gunning for me for a long time.'

He moved towards the door. 'What about the steak?' asked Jo.

'I'll be back, won't I?' he said. 'So don't go scoffing it.'

He went, returning momentarily to collect his cap and to wave a kiss to Jo, who turned the grill off, left the kitchen, closing the door, and walked across to Sister's office. As she crossed the corridor she heard someone moving about in the bathroom. She presumed it was a person though all she could actually hear was a chinking noise. She went to investigate, opening the door to see Mrs Khalid, an Indian or Pakistani patient (Jo was not sure which) performing her ablutions. The chinking noise was her jewellery rattling, particularly the many bangles on her wrists.

'What are you doing, Mrs Khalid?' asked Jo. It seemed a funny time for somebody to be washing themselves, quarter past twelve at night.

Mrs Khalid, whom Jo had never actually heard speak, just smiled broadly, shrugged her shoulders and continued washing her face and neck. Jo decided to let her get on with it. She was doing nobody any harm and so far as Jo knew it might have been an established Indian or Pakistani custom to wash your neck after midnight.

As she closed the bathroom door, Inspector Townsend appeared in the corridor. He was a very square man, especially in his uniform, which tended to be all horizontals – pockets, epaulettes and flat cap. He was very smart, plainly taking a great pride in his appearance, and his heavy, jowled face was rosy with cleanliness.

He spoke in a very thin voice for such a powerful man. He said, 'Ah, Nurse, I'm told one of my officers might be around here somewhere.' He waited, obviously expecting her to say that the policeman was in the toilet or in the office or somewhere.

'Officer? What officer's that?' said Jo, doing her impersonation of a doe. She went into the office. Inspector Townsend followed her, his little red eyes, surprising in such a big man, flicking round the room and even looking under the desk, Jo noticed.

'I was told he might be here,' said the Inspector, plainly a man not easily put off – which probably explained his rank. People who are not easily put off do tend to get on in the world.

'Why should he be here?' countered Jo, as she settled at the desk. She looked up at him and felt, despite the Inspector's size and his policeman's uniform, very self-possessed.

'His car's outside,' said the Inspector, with the air of a man not only producing a rabbit out of a hat but a whole litter as well.

'Well, I'm sorry,' said Jo, picking up a pen as if she had some work to do, which in fact she had not. 'His car may be outside, but *he's* not here. Have you tried Casualty? That's where you usually find policemen.'

Inspector Townsend looked at her for what seemed a very long time, his small eyes hardly moving. 'I see,' he suddenly squeaked, 'I see . . .' He turned abruptly and left. Jo was taken somewhat by surprise. She sat there staring after him until Mrs Parkinson appeared at the door, looking like a baby zeppelin, in a very short nightie and decorative boudoir slippers which were totally incongruous at the end of legs like hams.

'You know what's bloody going on I suppose, Nurse?' she accused Jo in her fishwife's voice. It was broad Cockney, high-pitched, and it never seemed to draw breath. It was very nearly in perpetual motion.

'Pardon?' asked Jo, pulling herself together to face this new adversary – for Mrs Parkinson was quite definitely adverse, and to the whole world, too.

'It's them bloody Pakis, isn't it?' she railed. (To Mrs Parkinson any coloured face from a mild coffee tan to a deep ebony was classified 'Paki'.) 'They're keeping us all awake, aren't they? Trotting about the bloody ward at this time of night like bloody zombies. Why can't they wash 'emselves when we all do? In the mornings? Too bloody high and mighty, that's their trouble! Think they're a cut above us lot. They think we're unclean, they do, they think we're unclean! Well, I'll tell you, I wouldn't let a bloody pig loose in some of their homes. And if they don't bloody like it here, they know what to do, don't they? You know one of 'em sleeps in her sari or whatever you call it, do you?'

'I've seen Mrs Khalid having a wash,' replied Jo when Mrs

Parkinson finally screeched to a temporary halt. 'But I haven't seen any of the others . . .'

'Well, you're the only bloody one who hasn't,' continued Mrs Parkinson, slipping into overdrive again virtually from the first syllable. 'They've all been washing their bleeding selves, waking us all up, trotting about jangling like Southend donkeys. Well it's got to stop. And I'll see it bloody does, don't you worry yourself, darling!'

She went. Jo was just about to sigh with relief when Mrs Parkinson immediately reappeared. For such a fat lady she could move with remarkable agility. 'And another thing, I've got bloody indigestion! And whose fault's that? That bloody chef's. Chef, he couldn't boil bloody water without burning it!'

'I'll give you . . .' began Jo. She was going to say '. . . something for it,' but Mrs Parkinson had vanished again. Jo decided she must ask Sister about the nocturnal habits of Mrs Khalid and her countrywomen; maybe they were something that Sister was familiar with, but they were certainly new to her.

The phone rang. It was Chris. 'Is he there?' he whispered in a seductive voice which, had Jo not known to whom it belonged, might have raised more than a passing interest.

'He's been and gone,' said Jo, whispering in her turn because whispering, like the 'flu, is infectious.

'You know what he's done? Blocked my car in with his. So I'm stuck.'

'What are you going to do?' asked Jo, genuinely concerned. 'He's obviously after your blood.'

'He is,' said Chris without a trace of worry. 'You've not scoffed my steak, have you?'

'No, 'course not.'

'Have you any bread?'

'Bread!' What does the maniac want bread for, puzzled Jo. 'Yes, 'she said.

'Well, put my steak between a couple of slices and I'll be up for it now.'

'Suppose you bump into your Inspector?'

'No chance, I'll be coming through the tunnel, won't I?' He hung up.

The 'tunnel' was an old corridor, old enough to be a secret passage really, running from the back of Male Medical to an outside stone staircase. It was an unofficial means of entry to or exit from the hospital which cut out the main entrance and bypassed the rather inquisitive porters. It was much beloved by people bent on secret errands or assignations. Jo herself had used it quite often and Julie Woods practically lived in it.

Jo hurried back to the kitchen, found a sliced loaf and some butter, buttered two slices and put one of the steaks between them, adding a pickled onion from her own private jar. Jo was very fond of pickled onions and also of olives, especially stuffed olives. She had been known to eat a whole jarful of stuffed olives during a single shift, much to the disgust of Ruth.

She had just finished the sandwich when Chris materialized beside her. It seemed to be a night for people materializing out of thin air, thought Jo. Mrs Khalid, the Inspector, Mrs Parkinson, and now Chris!

'Where is it?' he said. 'Nothing like being chased round a hospital for giving you an appetite. Nearly as good as being chased round a bedroom.' He seized the sandwich, took an enormous bite and, leaning casually against the sink as if he had not a care in the world, started to masticate gently, relishing every crumb, every shred of meat, every pocket of juice. Constable Jackson never did anything by halves.

'Supposing he comes back?' said Jo, not sharing his equanimity.

'Who cares?' shrugged Chris, swallowing and taking a second enormous bite out of his sandwich. 'Aren't you putting the kettle on?'

'You mean he's gone,' pressed Jo, attributing Chris's cool to his possibly knowing more than she did.

'Nope.'

'Then he might come back and find you. I told him I hadn't seen you, but he didn't look convinced.'

'Who cares?' said Chris, finally demolishing the sandwich completely. 'I'm dying for a cuppa, darling, I really am,' he said with his mouth full of food.

Jo was beginning to feel apprehensive. 'It's not just you, you know,' she said. 'I stand to get in trouble, if he finds you here. I mean he looks the sort who'd get a lot of pleasure out of telling Sister I've been entertaining a policeman in here.'

'He is and you have,' said Chris, obviously enjoying himself.

'Then beat it,' said Jo. 'Now!'

'All right,' said Chris, straightening up. 'But there's no need to worry, I've got Old Bonzo over a barrel. I'll be back for that cuppa.' And as he passed her on the way to the door he kissed her just on the corner of the mouth, which Jo found quite nice.

She decided to see how Mrs Parkinson was and whether Mrs Khalid had finished her ablutions. The bathroom was empty, which was a good sign and the ward, too, was now quiet enough. Mrs Khalid and the two other immigrant ladies in the ward were asleep or appeared to be. But when Jo reached Mrs Parkinson, last but one on the left, she found her awake and smoking.

'How's your indigestion?' asked Jo.

'Not so bad,' said Mrs Parkinson, who did not sound quite as aggressive as usual.

'Can't you sleep?'

'No.'

'Do you want a pill?'

'No.'

'Better sleeping than just lying there.'

'Got my own pill, haven't I?' said Mrs Parkinson, withdrawing from under the bedclothes a half-bottle of gin. 'Fancy a nip?' she asked Jo.

'No, no thanks,' said Jo, not all that surprised by the appearance of the bottle, because drinking by patients – and staff for that matter – was not entirely unknown in the hospital. It was only last month that she and Julie Woods had got quite squiffy one night on a bottle of sherry. It had been given to them by the husband of an American patient who came laden with gifts of booze, chocolates and cigarettes every time he visited his wife. She had broken her hip falling down an escalator in the Underground and he could not get over the fact she was being treated practically free; so he thought that the least he could do was to spread a little material joy and comfort among the hospital staff. He had also asked Nurse Johnson, an agency nurse who was generally recognized as quite the most glamorous lady at St Angela's, to go out for a meal with him some night. She declined because she had other fish to fry – such as Mr Asmara, a consultant, who was not only good-looking and well-off but had a wife who was safely back home in Sri Lanka.

Mrs Parkinson took a swig from her bottle. Despite her size she was a very sick woman. She had high blood pressure and a skin complaint which was causing some concern. Her weight was a problem, too, and she smoked too much, often breaking out into paroxysms of coughing which left her face puce-coloured. She was only thirty-eight, but looked fifty, particularly now when she was depressed, without even the energy to complain.

'What are the coppers doing round here?' she asked.

'It's a long story,' said Jo.

'Sniffing after you, are they darling?' Mrs Parkinson's eyes leered but only briefly. The sex urge is never altogether stilled even in someone as chronically sick as she was. 'Watch 'em, darling! Watch fellers! They'll promise you paradise to get what they want. Then afterwards . . . you're a chattel, darling, a bloody chattel.'

'I think you'd better give me the bottle,' said Jo. 'You shouldn't be drinking gin, you shouldn't be drinking anything.'

'Shouldn't . . .' sneered Mrs Parkinson, 'I shouldn't have been born, but I was.' Jo reached out and gently took the bottle from her. She did not resist, but she said, without a trace of emotion, 'I'll not get out of here, darling, not alive.' And she closed her eyes.

Jo returned to the kitchen suddenly feeling flat and sad herself. Normally a gay, outgoing personality, Jo had a serious weakness for a nurse. Her friendliness tended to lead to her becoming too much involved with her patients, involved too deeply not only in their medical problems but in their personal ones, too. The dangers of that are fairly obvious. A nurse, like a doctor or a policeman, must grow a second skin or the very nature of her job, with its recurring themes of disease, pain and death, would drive her mad. She must be naturally compassionate, but she must also remain detached and this not just for her own sake: the more detached she is the cooler she is, and the better she is able to make decisions – life and death decisions. Sister Easby in particular had tried to impress this upon Jo, who was trying hard to comply but every now and again there would be somebody who slipped through her defences and she would be lost again. Gross, aggressive, unprepossessing Mrs Parkinson had not actually slipped through yet, but she was nevertheless a pathetic human being without many friends and apparently without hope as well. Jo filled the kettle and switched it on, deliberately turning her thoughts to Ruth so that she would stop worrying about Mrs Parkinson. Ruth had come home for her tea that day in a quiet mood. Jo had asked her if there was anything wrong. 'Nothing I don't have to try and get over,' Ruth had replied enigmatically. Then she had asked, 'Do you think I'd make a good wife?'

' 'Course,' Jo had assured her, 'if you find the right feller.'

'Ah yes, the right feller! Mr Bloody Wonderful!' And Ruth had gone to bed at quarter to five in the afternoon.

Jo was part-way through her steak when Sister Framley appeared, in readiness for the Houseman's rounds, Jo presumed.

'Coping, are you, Nurse?' she asked, although it was pretty obvious that Jo was coping, otherwise she would have bleeped her.

'Yes, thank you, Sister,' said Jo, 'I took a bottle of gin off Mrs Parkinson. I wonder where she got it?'

'She's the sort who'd find herself a bottle of gin in the middle of the Sahara desert,' said Framley, rather unkindly thought Jo. 'Doctor Khan's up to his neck with a cardiac arrest in Male Surgical so you'll not be seeing him for some time. You're sure you're all right?'

'Fine,' said Jo.

'Right, I'll get back to the fray then. Where did you get that?' She indicated the partly eaten steak.

'Brought it with me, Sister,' lied Jo. 'I was feeling peckish so I thought I'd have a little snack. Everything being so quiet . . .'

'Some snack,' sniffed Sister Framley. 'I thought you girls could hardly afford to keep body and soul together.'

'Oh, it's a very special snack is this, Sister,' grinned Jo. 'Baked beans for the rest of the week.'

'Hmm,' said Framley, obviously not believing a word of it.

'What gets me is how you manage to keep your figure, all the eating you seem to do. I wish I could. My husband thinks I'd make a very good discus thrower!' And she left Jo to her steak, her reflections and to Female Medical.

She was not left undisturbed for long. Mrs Parkinson now came to ask for a couple of sleeping pills. She looked even worse, haggard and dribbling a little from one corner of her mouth. She assured Jo that she was not in any pain and her pulse and temperature were in fact normal for her. She also swore she had not drunk much gin. Indeed the bottle Jo had taken was hardly touched, so Jo gave her one pill and kept an eye on her until she was certain that she was asleep. She also inspected the immigrant women and sure enough one of them was sleeping in her sari, or something very like a sari: when Jo bent closer she was met with an unblinking stare from two large brown eyes which were neither friendly nor unfriendly; perhaps just a little frightened.

Inspector Townsend was waiting for her when she got back to the office. As soon as she walked through the door he squeaked, 'Where is he, Nurse?'

'Who?' asked Jo though with slightly less confidence than she had displayed in his presence previously, because he now seemed much more sure of himself, as though he had some new and vital information.

'You know who I mean,' said the Inspector, plainly trying to bore a hole through her eyes and through to her head with his own red ones, like some latter-day Sherlock Holmes.

'I don't,' said Jo. She sat down again because she felt more in control sitting down and less physically intimidated by him.

'I am satisfied that one of my officers is in this hospital,' he said, his voice suddenly very official despite its lack of decibels. 'And by reason of what I've been told, I am also satisfied that he has been in this ward. I want to make contact with this officer, so I'd be obliged if you would assist me in that endeavour.' Inspector Townsend could achieve a nice turn of phrase when he put his mind to it.

'Sorry,' said Jo, trying to make her voice sound assertive, 'but if he is in the hospital, I haven't seen him.'

That plainly made the Inspector very angry. His thick neck,

already constrained by his whiter-than-white shirt collar, swelled perceptibly so that a fold of flesh bulged over the rim of the collar – like dough, thought Jo. He said again, 'I see . . . I see. Well, I'll tell you this, missy. If I *do* find him, and I will, then you're in trouble. Dead trouble. With your Matron, who I happen to know very well. I ask a question, I expect it to be answered truthfully. And if it's not, well . . . we'll see, won't we, missy? We'll see . . .'

If he calls me missy once more, I'll hit him, thought Jo, her own temper rising. But he did not get the chance to. His personal radio came to life. 'Frederick Road to Inspector Townsend,' said a young voice in a very conversational tone. The Inspector switched to transmit. 'Inspector Townsend,' he replied curtly.

'Oh sir, it's four oh Jackson,' continued the voice. 'Seems he's returned to his car outside St Angela's to find your car there, sir, and you're blocking him in. He wondered if you needed any assistance or anything, sir.'

The silence that followed was louder than any explosion. Jo watched, fascinated, as Inspector Townsend struggled manfully to control burgeoning apoplexy and succeeded, though at the expense of yet another roll of flesh bulging over his collar. When he spoke into the radio, his voice was fairly controlled. He said very quietly, 'Tell Jackson to stop where he is. I'll come back to my car.'

'Right sir,' said the voice. 'Just one more thing, sir. Four oh's got a prisoner. A prowler.'

Jo could not quite suppress a giggle. Chris and his prowler! She would believe he had caught one when she saw him – or her.

Inspector Townsend switched off his radio. 'Do you mind telling me what it might be that's amusing you, Nurse?' he said, his voice squeaking again and his neck returning to normal.

'Nothing,' said Jo, pursing her lips to prevent another outburst. 'Just . . . something I thought about.'

'Yes well,' he said. 'Don't think you're heard the last of this, because you haven't. Not by a long chalk. I won't have flighty little pieces like you leading my officers astray.' He presumably thought that to be an adequate parting shot because he turned and walked out impressively.

The Inspector could barely have been out of earshot when Jo really gave vent to the giggles. She laughed as her mother did at Abbott and Costello and she was still giggling spasmodically half an hour later when Chris Jackson's bushy blond eyebrows bobbed into view round the kitchen door once again.

'How does half a dozen cream buns just out of the oven grab you?' he said, entering the kitchen and producing from his cornucopia of a tunic two paper bags each containing three cream buns.

'Oh no!' laughed Jo, quite exhausted by now. 'Where in heaven's name did you get those?'

'Fell out of a baker's van,' said Chris. 'Go down well with that cuppa I never did get.'

'God, don't you take the biscuit . . .'

'Sorry, no biscuits, only cream buns. Do I get that cuppa or don't I?'

'Where's your Inspector?'

'Gone back to the station in tears.'

Jo could very well believe that, remembering Inspector Townsend's anger and frustration. She filled the kettle and switched it on. She thought she heard someone moving in the ward and went to look, but nobody seemed to be in any particular distress. Even Mrs Parkinson was snoring gently, and she was smiling, too, which was very unusual.

When Jo returned to the kitchen Chris was on his second cream bun. The other four were laid out neatly on a plate and he had found the teabags and put them in two beakers. 'Didn't realize you were domesticated,' Jo twitted him.

'I'd make a perfect husband,' said Chris, licking flecks of cream from round his mouth, which Jo decided was quite sexy. 'I can cook, clean, sew buttons on and I'm dynamite in bed.'

'Why don't you get married, then?' asked Jo, actually knowing the answer because if ever there was a natural bachelor it was Chris Jackson. Tying him to marriage would be like caging a kestrel.

'I'm trying to find the perfect wife, aren't I? By process of selection. And it's a long process. Would you like to apply? Be a very rewarding experience, even if you didn't get the job.'

'Can't you be serious about anything?'

'I am serious, deadly serious.'

'I don't mean about that.'

He looked at her over his third cream bun, his pale blue eyes suddenly grave. He said, 'I'm serious about the job.'

'You don't give that impression,' said Jo, pouring water from the kettle into the beakers.

'No, I am, really I am,' insisted Chris. 'I might lark about a bit, have some fun with berks like Bonzo. But I'm a good copper. I know my patch, I know a lot of people who would do me a favour and what's most important I know the villains and they know me. And I've nicked a lot of them, too. I enjoy being a copper. Every day something different. If you look for it anyway. I wouldn't change my job for Miss World. Just like you wouldn't change yours.'

'Who says I wouldn't?' asked Jo, handing him his tea and taking a cream bun herself. They were still warm and very, very good.

'Would you?'

Jo thought for a second, but that was all. 'No,' she said. 'Oh, I've considered changing it. I still do. But I wouldn't. 'Less I get the sack, which is highly likely.'

'Tell you what, though,' said Chris.

'What?'

'Nurses and coppers. We get on well together, don't we? Well, we both know what it's all about.'

'You proposing, Chris Jackson?' said Jo, fluttering her eyelashes and eating her cream bun.

'Not yet,' he said and Jo decided his voice was serious as well as his expression.

She asked, as much just to change the subject as anything, 'Did you really catch a prowler tonight?'

'Oh yes,' he said. 'Straight up.'

'Where?'

'Just outside the entrance.'

'Who was he?'

'Well, as it turned out, he was a foreigner. Couldn't speak much English or at least he pretended he couldn't.'

A terrible thought was taking shape inside Jo's head.

'What kind of foreigner?' she asked, her eyes narrowing.

'Just a foreigner,' said Chris, far too innocently.

'Chris!' she warned him. 'What kind of foreigner?'

'French,' admitted Chris, grinning like an idiot. 'Called himself Raoul or something.'

'You rotten . . .! Where is he?'

'Oh, I sent him packing,' said Chris, picking up his tea. 'He wasn't much of a prowler.'

He nonchalantly took a sip of his tea as Jo started to giggle again, uncontrollably this time, while in the ward Mrs Parkinson snored.

St. Angela's Hospital

MERICI ROAD
LONDON S.W. 11

HOSPITAL SCHOOL OF NURSING
CONFIDENTIAL REPORT

Surname Rutherford **Forenames** Patricia Anne

Date of birth 23/6/54 **Expected date of final examination** Autumn 1978

Previous nursing or other relevant qualifications None

Confidential report

Patricia has previously attempted a teachers' training course, but gave it up as she decided that teaching was not the right career for her. Her father is a company director and her mother belongs to several local welfare charities. Patricia is an only child. At her preliminary interview, she struck me as being an intelligent, confident girl, and her first few weeks of training have confirmed this. She does, however, find difficulty in accepting some of the disciplines involved in nurse training and taking instructions from her seniors. As yet she has shown little sympathy for the patient, but then for the most part she has been in the classroom; this may well change when she goes on the ward. To sum up, Patricia has all the intelligence and initiative required, but her rather over-confident attitude needs modifying if she is to work well within the ward team. Hopefully this will be remedied during her training.

Heather Windrup

Heather Windrup, Senior Nursing Tutor

PATRICIA I had a teacher at school who once told me that everything that happens to you happens for a reason, and therefore must be good. I had just failed to get into my first choice of university at the time, and she caught me in the classroom one evening, biting back angry tears of disappointment. She said that one day I'd look back on it, and realize that it had happened for the best and be glad. I found her philosophy as difficult to swallow then as I do now and yet I suppose there is a kind of odd logic in it. It makes comforting sense out of the apparently inexplicable blows one receives in life, and gives one's existence a purpose, if there is some determinate, guiding hand, helping one along . . .

It's difficult to know where my story actually starts. I tried to isolate one particular moment, and say, 'yes, the whole thing can be traced back to that one moment in time.' But it wasn't that easy. I'm afraid that wherever I begin, I'll be leaving out some vital part, some basic ingredient that the experienced storyteller would seize upon and build into the beginning of his tale. Yet mine isn't a tale, or even a story. It's more a collection of events . . . I suppose a logical place to begin is that Friday afternoon when Miss Windrup, our Nursing Tutor, kept me back after class.

It was raining outside and it seemed as if we'd been shut in that classroom for hours. Windy was giving a practical demonstration about the removal of dressings after operations. I was sitting in the back row, wondering what I was going to do with myself that weekend. Maureen Morahan, another first-year I generally knocked around with, was doing a brief ward stint, so I would be on my own. I found myself sighing, and Miss Windrup glanced at me over the rows of heads.

'Yes, Nurse?'

I jerked upright. 'I didn't speak, Miss Windrup.'

'Oh, I thought you did.' She looked at me for a moment. 'I'm not boring you, I hope?'

'Oh no, Miss Windrup.'

'I'm relieved to hear it.'

I crouched lower in my seat and looked at my watch. Only

another couple of minutes to go. When the class was finally over, we all stood up, stretching ourselves. Miss Windrup stood at her desk, putting her things away, and as we filed past, we all went through the ritual of calling out goodnight. My turn came and I politely wished her a nice weekend, and was just moving towards the door when she called my name. I stood still for a minute, and then turned to face her.

'Yes, Miss Windrup?'

'I want a word with you, Nurse. Have you a moment now?'

'Well ...' I glanced at the other girls, gleefully disappearing out of the classroom door.

'It won't take long,' Miss Windrup said in her 'we're all equals together' voice. She waved me to a seat and continued to roll up the dressings she had used during her demonstration.

'I really want to have a chat with you. Find out how you're feeling about things.'

'Things?'

'Your training, for instance.' She flashed me what was supposed to be a reassuring smile. 'Call it a progress report if you like. I do it with all the girls. Nothing written down on paper – I just like to chat things over, and if there are any problems, see if I can do anything.'

'I see.' I waited for her to go on.

'And of course,' she gave me another smile, 'if I think there is any cause for concern, it gives me the opportunity to point it out.'

A measured pause followed. She was still winding up the dressings with expert ease. Keeping my eyes on her hands, I asked in an even voice, 'And is there cause for concern, Miss Windrup?'

She hesitated. 'Not *concern* so much. Apprehension possibly.'

'Over me?'

'Over aspects of you, anyway.' She put the dressings down and crossed to sit next to me. 'Tell me something, Patricia,' she asked in a curious voice. 'Why did you decide to go in for nursing?'

'I wanted to help people.'

'You could have gone into social work and done that.'

'Yes, well ... I've always wanted to be a nurse, I suppose,' I said rather lamely.

'Hmm.' She shot me a disbelieving glance before returning to her dressings. For a moment I thought the interview was at an end, but then she suddenly turned to me.

'I only ask because of your attitude. Now take Maureen Morahan, for example. Nursing was obviously a childhood ambition with her, it shows in everything she does. Her enthusiasm, her attention to detail. Whereas you . . .' She glanced at me, searching for the words. 'You're more impatient. I know you're anxious to start on the wards proper, but your anxiety often seems like restlessness and truculence.'

'I don't mean to give that impression.' I twisted round in my seat. 'It's just being stuck in a classroom again, like school . . .'

'But if you don't pay attention, you won't be ready to go onto the wards. Then you'll be "stuck in the classroom" as you call it for yet another session.'

'I do pay attention!' I replied rather hotly. 'I've always done well in the tests.'

'I'm talking about attitude, Nurse,' she said in a pointed tone. 'Your exam results are, as you say, very good. But you give the impression of being indolent and lazy. You don't immediately strike one as being a . . .' – once again she paused – 'caring person. That's why I asked you about your motives for going into nursing. They aren't immediately apparent, I'm afraid.'

'Just because I don't fit into the conventional mould doesn't mean to say I won't be a good nurse, does it?'

She studied me carefully for a minute. 'No, it doesn't. And I think you could make a good nurse. If you'd just . . . modify your manner a bit. Learn a bit of humility. You've only just started your training, you can't possibly know all the answers yet, so be guided by those who do. If you think I lean on you rather hard, just think what it'll be like when you start on the ward. You'll have ward sisters and staff nurses breathing down your neck all the time. Taking orders is something you're just going to have to get used to, I'm afraid.'

I didn't know what to say to that, so I said nothing. I glanced up at the clock behind her. It was fifteen minutes to five. I looked back at Miss Windrup, who was watching me with a wry smile.

'You're obviously anxious to be off. We'll continue our chat some other time.'

'Yes, Miss Windrup.' I stood up and made for the door. Then a thought suddenly struck me, and I turned back.

'Miss Windrup?'

'Yes, Nurse?'

'What exactly did you mean, modify my manner?'

She didn't speak for a moment. She looked very small in that classroom, surrounded by rows of chairs and desks.

'Think about it, Patricia,' she said in an oddly evasive voice. 'I'm sure you can work it out.'

As I say, that conversation took place at around five in the evening. I left Miss Windrup, rather disturbed by her last remark, and I started to make my way towards the nurses' home. In the courtyard I caught sight of Maureen, speeding along to the main gate. I shouted to her, and she pulled up, looking towards me distractedly.

'Where are you off to?' I shouted as I panted up to her.

'I'm going to have tea with me Auntie Kath.' She looked faintly anxious, her normally placid face tense and drawn.

'What's up?' I asked, linking my arm through hers. 'Not still homesick, are you?'

She shot me a quick glance and looked away. 'You always have to make a joke of everything, Pat.'

'Sorry.'

We walked along in silence for a minute, Maureen keeping her face slightly averted from me. I shot a sideways glance at her.

'You really miss it, don't you?'

'Yes.' She said it in an extraordinarily simple way, as if she was just talking about the weather, and it suddenly struck me how vulnerable Maureen was. She seemed so guileless compared with me. I suppose that was one of the reasons we were friends. I'd always felt oddly drawn to her. She aroused some protective instinct in me that I never knew I had.

We parted at the entrance of the hospital and I watched her hop on a bus before turning back towards the nurses' home. The prospect of a lonely Friday night loomed heavily before me, and as I walked along I kept passing groups of nurses, all dressed up and obviously on their way out somewhere . . .

When I first entered my room in the nurses' home, I didn't notice anything was different. I flung myself on the bed and started to flick through my address book, wondering who I could ring up and fix a date with. I was lying there, sprawled on the bed, when I happened to notice the chest of drawers. At first nothing much registered. I just looked at it, in passing as it were, without drawing any conclusions. Then it suddenly struck me. All the drawers were open, and the contents sagging out. For a moment I didn't move. I just lay there, looking at the chest, trying to recollect if I had left it in that state in the morning. I got up and crossed over to it. Then, all at once, a wave of nausea hit me. Someone had been going through my things. The clothes were all flurried about, as if whoever it was had been searching for something in great haste.

It's a difficult feeling to describe, if you've never experienced it. The sensation of being defiled. The outrage when you realize that someone – some unknown person – has been rifling through your belongings . . . but the outrage is shortlived. I suppose because it's impotent, because you don't know whom to aim it at. And in its place comes repulsion. That's what I felt at that moment, looking at my clothes strewn across the drawers. Suddenly I didn't want to wear any of those clothes again, because some filthy, alien hand had been touching them . . .

After a few minutes I collected myself. I was obviously the victim of a petty thief. This kind of thing is pretty frequent in hospitals. Every week you hear of someone who's had their purse lifted, or a patient complaining because someone's been through their locker. A hospital must be paradise to a thief. He just has to don a white overall and he has access everywhere. All the wards, Casualty, the canteens, wherever he thinks it might be lucrative to go.

I remembered I'd passed Sister Broomstock, the home sister, in her office on my way in, so I charged down the stairs to see her. I knocked on the door and walked straight in. She was seated at her desk, filling out some forms.

'I've been robbed,' I said in a carefully controlled voice. 'Someone's been in my room and gone through my things.'

She swivelled around in her seat, peering at me through her winged spectacles. She didn't speak, but abruptly stood up and, picking up a huge bunch of keys, marched off up the corridor. I tagged along behind until we reached my room. The door was still open and she swiftly entered, casting an efficient look around.

'What's missing?' she asked in her brassy Scots accent.

'Missing?'

'What did they take?'

I stared back at her stupidly. In my shock at the discovery, and my haste to report the intruder, I'd failed to check what had actually been stolen.

'I'm not sure.'

'Look then, girl.'

Taking my key, I unlocked the desk drawers where I kept my odd bits of jewellery. I made a rapid check; everything was there. Then I moved to the wardrobe. The fur coat Daddy had given me for Christmas was still hanging inside, as well as my camel-hair jacket and velvet trouser suit. Feeling Sister's cold eye on me, I moved to the chest of drawers. I hesitated a moment before quickly examining the contents of each drawer.

'I don't understand it,' I said finally. 'It's all there.'

'You said you'd been robbed.'

'I thought I had!' I pointed to the chest of drawers. 'Look at that, someone's been through it . . .'

She moved to the chest and, without touching anything, looked at the sagging drawers.

'You probably left it like it this morning.'

'I most certainly didn't!' I picked up some shirts from the top drawer and turned to her. 'I don't even keep these there. I always have them in the middle drawer, with my sweaters. Someone's been in here, I tell you.'

'Was the door locked?'

'Of course. I unlocked it when I came back.'

'How d'you suggest whoever it was got in, then?'

I hesitated fractionally. 'Perhaps someone got hold of your pass key.'

'I hold the pass key,' she reminded me rather coldly. 'And I don't let it out of my sight.'

'Well, I don't know, Sister. But they got in all right ...' I glanced at the chest, at the sagging drawers and at my jumble of clothes. 'I know someone's been going through my things. I can feel it.'

Sister Broomstock didn't speak for a minute. Her huge bulk seemed to fill the tiny room, and she just stood there, the keyring in her hand, looking around.

'Well,' she said at last, 'since nothing's been taken, I'm not sure what you expect me to do.'

She doesn't believe me, I thought. She doesn't believe a word I'm saying. I sat down on the bed and looked at her.

'I am telling the truth, Sister. Someone has been in here.'

She smiled a crooked sort of smile at me. 'I once had a similar experience,' she said in a sing-song sort of voice. 'It was years ago. I was studying for an exam, and sleeping very badly. Every morning I noticed the window was open, yet I knew I'd shut it before I went to sleep. I was convinced someone had been in my room. Some kind of peeping tom who climbed through the window and sat by my bed, watching me sleep. You know who it turned out to be?'

I shook my head. She moved to the window and wiped it with the flat of her hand. Then she turned back to me.

'It was me,' she said. 'Every night I got up and opened the window in my sleep. Extraordinary, isn't it?'

I looked at her for a second. 'Are you suggesting that *I* did this, Sister? In my sleep?'

'Not at all.' She smiled briskly and crossed to the door. 'But you might well have left it in that state this morning and forgotten all about it. After all, you're not the tidiest of girls, are you, dear?' And she went, quietly closing the door behind her.

Naturally I was furious. My anger at the actual incident seemed meagre compared with the fury I felt towards Sister Broomstock and her disbelieving attitude. However, after a couple of days I forgot all about it. Memory does that – have you noticed? If something painful happens, it's not willpower or any kind of conscious effort that steps in to erase the experience, it's memory. Or rather, the weakness of it. Gradually the painful image becomes blurred, the picture smudges and is finally lost. And that's what happened over my so-called intruder. I simply forgot all about it.

But then on the Monday something else happened. I'd spent the morning with Miss Windrup in the classroom as usual. We'd had a physiology seminar, and the classroom was so cold that I'd shivered all the way through it. When the lunchbreak came I decided to pop up to my room to collect my cardigan. Outside my door I scrabbled around in my pocket for my key, and was just about to insert it, when I realized that the door was ajar. Cautiously I pushed it open and entered my room. It was empty, and at first glance seemed in pretty much the same state as when I had left it that morning. Then I caught sight of the dressing table. I kept various pictures on it, you know the type of thing, framed prop-up photographs of my family, friends and so on. I suppose there must have been about half a dozen of them in all. Anyway, something about that dressing table struck me as odd. There was something unfamiliar and different about it. Then I realized what it was. The pictures were all lying flat on their faces. Someone had been in, and put every photograph face down on the dressing table . . .

I was standing there, staring at the dressing table, when Jenny Sorrell, a West Indian girl in my tutorial set, passed by the door. I suppose the sight of me standing there, rooted to the spot, must have arrested her attention, because she pulled up and came in.

'Coming down to lunch, then?' she asked, glancing at me curiously.

I dragged my eyes off the dressing table, and turned to look at her.

'Pat?' She touched my arm briefly, in a tiny gesture of concern. 'What is it? What's happened?'

It seemed such a stupid, petty thing when I tried to put it into words. Like when you were at school, and you tried to recount some playground incident to your parents. You could see them give you attention, because it was obviously important to you, but their minds were far away, on some elevated adult subject. That's what it was like telling Jenny Sorrell about my apparent intruder. I told her about the chest of drawers, about the open door and photographs, and she listened intently, her serious brown eyes on my face. Yet I could tell that her mind was on other things. Probably on the lunch queue in the canteen, or how well she'd done in the anatomy test . . . When I'd finished she just stood there, her eyes still pinned on my face. I abruptly stood up and mechanically started propping up the photographs again.

'What are you doing?' Jenny asked in surprise.

'What does it look like?' I replied sourly.

'Shouldn't you leave them?' she queried in a puzzled tone. 'For Sister Broomstock to see?'

'She doesn't believe me any more than you do, so what's the point?'

'Who says I don't believe you!'

'I do.' I propped up the last of the photographs and turned to face her.

'You think I'm making the whole thing up, don't you?'

She looked uncomfortable for a minute, then a look of defiance crossed her face, like a schoolgirl who's been caught out, and who decides that attack is the best form of defence.

'You must admit it's pretty peculiar. I mean, supposing someone did get in, why didn't they take anything? And what's the point of tampering with a few photographs?' She threw the question out like a challenge. 'It doesn't make sense. A much more likely explanation is that you left your door open this morning before going to the seminar, and it created some kind of draught . . .' She gestured vaguely around the room. 'And it knocked the pictures down.'

'All of them?' I asked dryly.

She shrugged. 'Why not?'

I looked at her for a moment and made a decision. Picking up my cardigan I moved to the door. Jenny swivelled round, watching me.

'Where are you going?'

'To eat,' I replied with a sweet smile. 'You're probably right.

It was more than likely the draught. Come on, or there'll be no decent food left.'

We were silent on our way to the canteen. A kind of chill had fallen over our relationship. On my part, there was a sense of disappointment. Jenny's obvious disbelief was a sign of her distrust in me, and that kind of distrust plants a splinter of doubt in a friendship ... On Jenny's part? Well, she was obviously puzzled and slightly disturbed by both my story and my behaviour. I had decided to agree with her simply because I couldn't bear her doubt another moment. And my sudden switch had left her bewildered and ill-at-ease.

When we collected our food trays we parted company. I watched Jenny's ample figure make its way up the aisle between the tables to join a group at the far end, while I turned off to the right, looking around for a familiar face. I soon found one. Susan Koppen, another girl in my tutorial group, was sitting on her own by the door. I moved over and stood in front of her.

'Okay if I join you?'

She looked up in surprise. Susan is an irritating kind of girl. She's one of those very blonde people, practically an albino I suppose, even her eyelashes are blonde. But that's not why she's irritating. She's irritating because she's so terribly placid. She has this sort of limp manner and doe-like expression. I can't remember where her home is now. Somewhere south of the river I think – Orpington or Herne Hill, somewhere like that. Somewhere unobtrusive and dull. And that's what Susan was, I suppose. Dull. It seems cruel to say it, but I'm trying to be honest. It's no good my writing down that I felt Susan had some poignant charm, some hidden attraction, because I don't think she had. She just seemed, well ... dull. She had these vacant blue eyes, which looked odd because of the blonde eyelashes. Her complexion was always slightly damp and pale, with a half-hearted sprinkling of freckles over her nose. Her hair was short, and viciously cut in a pageboy bob.

Anyway, I sat down opposite her and started to eat. My mind was still going over my conversation with Jenny Sorrell: I suppose I was still inwardly enraged because it seemed no one would believe me. Looking back on it I realize that it was that prompted me into talking to Susan. Instinctively I knew she was incapable of disbelief or doubt, and at that moment, all I wanted was someone to listen. Even if that someone was only Susan Koppen . . . I glanced across at her. She was eating with her head bent low over her plate.

'Susan?'

For a second I thought she hadn't heard. Then she looked up at me, and something stirred at the back of those vacant blue eyes. A flicker of something that came and went so fast, you wondered if it was ever there.

'Yes?'

I looked at her earnest, expectant face and the urge to confide in her ebbed away. Maybe Jenny was right, maybe the whole thing had happened as she said. Maybe it was the draught that had knocked the pictures over. And after all, nothing had been taken, so where was the harm? I smiled dismissively at Susan.

'It's okay. It doesn't matter.'

She gave me a last, lingering look before returning to her food. I leaned back in my chair and looked across the tables to where Jenny and the others were sitting, their heads bent together in animated conversation, with cigarette smoke hanging in a cloud above them. With a guilty nod at Susan, I abruptly picked up my tray and went over to join them . . .

Before describing the next events, I suppose I should try to convey my feelings to the reader. I wasn't frightened, that would be putting it too strongly. I just felt wary, and rather disturbed. But the disbelief shown by Jenny Sorrell, and indeed by everyone I had attempted to tell about it, soon pervaded my own reaction to the incidents, and eventually I dismissed them from my mind.

Perhaps there is something else I should try to put across at this stage . . . That is, how I fitted in at the nurses' home and at the training school itself. Without this information it might be difficult for you to fit the pieces together and my story won't make sense.

The minimum, and by and large average, age of entry into nursing training is eighteen. So Jenny Sorrell, Susan Koppen, Maureen Morahan and the rest were all eighteen, or at most nineteen. And then there was me, at the grand old age of twenty-one. I expect that three-year age gap doesn't mean much to you, but it means a lot to me. The acute experiences you cram into that intervening period prove to have a profound influence on the way your character is to be moulded. For most of the others it was their first break with home. Their first uncertain steps into the outside world, where independence means taking your own decisions, and the grim realization that few people give a damn whether those decisions are the right ones or not . . . It's a sink-or-swim sort of situation. You either put a bold face on it all, and strike out with confidence, or else you go along more hesitantly, quietly feeling your way and developing your opinions. Well, I'd been through all that, you see. I'd made the initial break with home some two years before when I went to a teachers' training college in Bristol. I'd returned home to live with my parents a year later, having chucked in the training college, but the break had been made. I was able to view both myself and my family with objectivity, and in doing so, to discover my own individuality. And I really carried that individuality around like a flag, waving it at whoever happened to be present.

I suppose I was rather patronizing to Maureen and the rest, because they seemed so young to me, with their half-formed ideas and their unquestioning surrender to the disciplines imposed on us by the senior nurses. Looking back on it, I wonder how they put up with me. But it was a front on my part. That kind of assured bravado always is. Very often I'd find myself envying Maureen's quiet conviction and sturdy sense of vocation. As I said, she had the sort of innocence that means you can commit yourself wholeheartedly to something and expect very little in return. It seems to become increasingly difficult, even at twenty-one, to commit yourself to anything. Perhaps because one's guileless enthusiasm has gone and scepticism has set in.

It was two more days before anything else happened. That would make it about Wednesday. We'd spent the day in the classroom with Miss Windrup and Mrs Smart, one of our other nursing tutors, and in the evening I persuaded a bunch of us to go off and see the latest Warren Beatty film. It must have been around eleven by the time we got back. There were four of us in all, Jenny Sorrell, Maureen Morahan, Sarah Regan and myself.

We larked around in the bus coming home, and by the time we arrived at the hospital we were all in a kind of high-pitched, hysterical, giggly state. We went into one of the communal kitchens in the nurses' home and started to cook ourselves a fry-up.

I suppose we must have been making a bit of a racket, because no sooner had we cracked some eggs and started to fry them than Sister Broomstock arrived on the scene. She had on one of those quilted dressing gowns and her hair stood out in clumps on her head, where she'd obviously wrenched off her curlers before hurtling down the corridor to sort us out. She stood in the doorway for a minute, surveying us coldly. Jenny Sorrell was giving us a demonstration of how she could crack an egg with one hand, and she was just completing her performance when her eye caught sight of Sister Broomstock. Our giggles faded away and for a moment the room fell perfectly quiet, save for the fat crackling in the frying pan.

'Well,' said Sister Broomstock finally, drawing her quilted dressing gown around her. 'This is a fine carry-on. You do realize that there are people trying to sleep here, don't you, and you've probably succeeded in waking them all up?'

We all eyed each other, choking back the giggles. Jenny Sorrell noisily made great play out of blowing her nose in an elaborate attempt to cover up the fact that she was laughing. The Broomstick crossed to the cooker and switched off the gas.

'All right,' she said, turning back to us. 'Off you go to bed now. You can clear this lot up in the morning.'

'What about our food, Sister?' I asked pointedly.

'You can eat it tomorrow, Nurse. It won't be wasted. Now, go on to bed, all of you.'

One by one we filed out of the kitchen and started towards our rooms.

What happened next has got a bit confused in my mind: but I do remember thinking how inaccurate old movies are when the heroine confronts a body lying on the floor. Cinema and television will have it that the heroine lets out a bloodcurdling scream, clasping both hands to her mouth. In fact when you receive a shock I'm inclined to think you're just numbed into silence. Not that my shock was anything like seeing a body sprawled across the floor, but it *was* a shock nonetheless.

I said a whispered goodnight to Jenny and Maureen and unlocked the door of my room and entered. Of course, to start with I didn't see anything because the light was still off. I pulled off my coat and flung it on the bed and crossed to the bedside lamp. And then I looked casually about the room. It was in total chaos. Every drawer was open and my clothes either hanging out, or strewn across the floor. Even the wardrobe was open and my coats lying limply at the bottom of it. All the books, usually kept in the desk in the corner, were scattered about, and the general effect was one of complete wreckage, as if some huge hand had entered the room and wrenched every object out of its rightful place and flung it as far away as possible . . . I stood by the bedside light, my hand still resting on the switch, looking around. I became aware of an odd, rasping sound in the room, and just as I was about to be clutched by panic – I realized that it was my own breathing that I could hear. It was then that I became aware of the smell. At first I didn't notice it. I suppose I was too dazed, but gradually I began to be aware of it. It was a pungent, stale sort of smell, yet not stale . . . Then it struck me what it was. It was the smell of scorching.

I can't quite remember what happened after that. I can remember that sensation, when I first realized what the smell was, but after that it gets a bit blurred. I didn't faint, if that's what you're thinking, but I must have run out of the room, because the next thing I remember is pounding down the corridor to Sister Broomstock's room at the end of the passage. I suppose one look at my face was enough for the Broomstick. She flung open her door, all ready to reprimand me for banging on her door in such a fashion, when suddenly her expression changed. It must have been because of something she saw in my face. I started to tell her about my room, about the clothes and the smell, but the words got all jumbled together in my excitement. The next thing I knew she was firmly grasping my arm and steering me down the corridor towards my room.

I think what she saw there took even her aback. She pulled up abruptly in the doorway and drew in her breath. The room was as I had left it. It looked forlorn in the harshness of the centre light, my clothes all hanging out of the drawers and draped across the floor.

'Good God.' Sister Broomstock gradually exhaled her breath. She slowly looked around the room, her hand still clutching my elbow.

'Shall we call the security officer?' I asked.

'I think we better had.' She wrinkled her nose. 'What's that smell?'

'I'm not sure. It's like . . .' I broke off and we looked at each other.

'Scorching.' Sister Broomstock relaxed her grip on my arm and crossed to the chest of drawers. She looked down at my clothes, tentatively picking up a shirt between her thumb and forefinger. Then, abruptly, she dropped it and turned to face me.

'Go and get the security officer,' she said in a harsh tone. 'And hurry!'

I don't know what she saw that made her use that tone, but I didn't need telling twice. A second later I was speeding off down the corridor to find Mr Neil, the security officer.

Nothing much happened after that. Not for a while anyway. Mr Neil and Sister Broomstock shut themselves in my room while I sat in the kitchen sipping tea. I was pretty tired by that time, and the glare of the neon light reflecting on the chrome surfaces in the kitchen made my eyes ache. It's odd, but I thought about absolutely nothing as I sat there on my own. I suppose I was shaken up, and in a kind of numbed state. I just sat there, at the table, looking at a fly slowly walking across the blue formica surface of the table, my mind a complete blank. Of course what I was really doing was stopping myself thinking about my room, and what was going on in there . . .

A few minutes later Sister Broomstock and Mr Neil came into the kitchen. Mr Neil was what you might call a typical security officer. He was an ex-policeman, with a strong back and a military bearing. He was getting on for sixty, I suppose, with watery blue eyes and a small, bristly moustache. He was in charge of all the security in the hospital, and when we'd first arrived he had given us a lecture on security. He came into the room and sat down opposite me, placing his well-manicured hands flat on the table.

'What a very distressing experience for you,' he said in a surprisingly gentle voice. I nodded mutely and waited for him to go on. He cleared his throat in an official sort of way and glanced at Sister Broomstock.

'I'm going to have to ask you a few questions, my dear. If you're up to it.'

I nodded again and he smiled at me reassuringly.

'It won't take long, and we might as well get it over with, mightn't we?' Behind him Sister Broomstock leant against the cooker and folded her arms, watching me impassively through her winged spectacles. Mr Neil took out a small, hardbacked notebook and carefully found a clean page. Then he pulled out a pencil and wrote the time and date on the top right-hand corner of the page. Then the questions began. What time had I come in? Did I touch anything? Had anything like this happened before? I told him about the two occasions, about the chest of drawers and the photographs. He listened intently, scribbling it all down in his notebook, occasionally licking his pencil between words. Eventually he leant back in his chair and looked at me with his mild blue eyes.

'And have you any idea, Nurse, who would want to do such damage?'

'Damage?'

He and the Broomstick exchanged a quick glance, and he cleared his throat again.

'Your clothes have been quite severely mutilated, I'm afraid. I only hope you took the precaution of being insured.'

'Mutilated!'

'Whoever it was . . .' He hesitated, watching me closely. 'Burnt holes in your clothes, most of your clothes I'm afraid, with a cigarette end. Some items are quite beyond repair.'

I stared at him blankly. So that was the scorching smell.

'Now have you any idea who would wish to do this to you?' he prompted gently.

'You mean . . .' I glanced up at Sister Broomstock and then

back to Mr Neil. 'Are you trying to tell me that it's someone I know who has done this?'

'It looks very much like it.' He started counting the facts off on his fingers. 'Fact one, it's nigh on impossible for an outsider to get into the nurses' home at any time of day, let alone night. Fact two, there is no sign of breaking and entering, suggesting that whoever it was had a key, or access to one, and judging by the locks on the doors of all the rooms, they're probably quite interchangeable . . .' He paused a moment, his eyes on my face. 'And lastly, none of the incidents involve theft. It's unlikely that an outside intruder, once having made his entrance, would simply leave without taking anything.'

The room fell silent. Suddenly I felt very cold. I shivered and Sister Broomstock cast me a concerned look.

'Perhaps these questions could be continued in the morning, Mr Neil,' she said, crossing to stand behind me. 'We're all too tired to think straight now.'

'Just one or two more things I'd like to ask, Sister. Then you can be on your way.'

'I can't go back in there!' For a moment I wondered who it was who had spoken out with such vehemence. Then I realized that it was me.

'Of course not. You can have the room next to mine. Then I can keep an eye on you.' Sister Broomstock patted my shoulder reassuringly. 'If you could just make it as quick as possible, Mr Neil.'

'Certainly.' He glanced down at his notebook, then back up to me. One of his eyes was watering, and a weary tear gently trickled down his cheek. The tear came to the network of wrinkles under his eye and then split, each part continuing down its own little inlet.

'You never answered my question,' Mr Neil said, reaching for a hankie, and wiping the tear away. 'So I can assume that you have no idea who would want to do this to you?'

'None.'

'You've no . . . enemies?'

'Enemies!' It sounded like an expression from a cheap television film.

'Anyone you don't get on with. Someone you might have . . .' He paused, trying to find the words. 'Snubbed or inadvertently angered. It does happen, you know.'

'Mr Neil.' I stood up and took my cup to the sink. 'I may not be the most popular girl here, but I can't see that's grounds for someone to . . .' I broke off, unable to put into words what I'd seen in my room.

'Quite so.' He looked down at his notebook and scribbled something down. 'So as far as you are aware, you've no particular enemies amongst the girls here, and you've no idea as to who would want to do such a thing?'

'None whatsoever.'

'Yes, well . . .' He snapped his notebook shut and stood up. 'That's it for now, then. Sister Broomstock will find you another room, and in the meantime, I wouldn't go into your room. I'll want another look around in the morning, and we might well get the police to have a look at it.'

'The police?'

'Just for the record.' He turned to Sister Broomstock. 'Right, then, Sister. I'll see you in the morning. Keep that door locked, won't you?'

'I will, Mr Neil. Goodnight.'

'Goodnight.' He turned to me. 'Goodnight, my dear.'

Sister Broomstock put me into an empty room next to hers. It was cold and had an unlived-in feeling, and the sheets felt icy to my touch. I couldn't stop shivering. I suppose the shock was affecting me physically, because mentally I still hadn't allowed myself to face up to it. Gradually, however, as the night progressed, the reality of it all began to strike me, and strike hard. At first all I could think of was my lovely clothes, all mutilated and scarred. I remembered the coat my father had given me. An expensive camel-hair jacket, with a red silk lining. I had caught a glimpse of it when Sister Broomstock and I had returned briefly to my room to collect a nightgown. It was lying in the bottom of the wardrobe, and even as it lay there, in a crumpled heap, I could see the scorch rings of the cigarette end branded into the soft fabric. Actually, I think it was the sight of that coat that disturbed me most. There was something particularly cruel about those little circular scorch marks, as well as something menacing and vicious . . . As if the burn marks were the physical manifestation of someone's hatred for me. For the first time I felt frightened. It was peculiar being in this new room, without any of my own things surrounding me, and all at once I felt very vulnerable and alone. I felt as if someone had jerked a carpet away from underneath me, and I was falling through space . . . I turned over in bed and clenched my teeth to stop them from chattering. If it had been a straightforward theft it would have been so much easier to accept . . . I remembered my conversation with Mr Neil and his conviction that it was someone I knew. I flung myself on my back and shut my eyes. Someone I knew. And with that thought in my mind, I drifted off into an uneasy sleep . . .

The next morning Sister Broomstock held a meeting. She assembled us all in the communal kitchen and made a rather pompous announcement about it all. She didn't go into much detail, just explained in her factual way what had happened, and said that if anybody knew anything, she'd like to see them.

I was standing next to her, and I found myself scrutinizing all the girls' faces. Most of them looked pretty shocked by what she had to say, and they kept casting me curious glances, as if trying to assess why such a thing should happen to me, and, more interesting still, how I was taking it.

When Sister Broomstock had finished her speech we all drifted down to the canteen for breakfast. On the way I was promptly surrounded by a group of the girls, led by Maureen and Jenny, all cross-questioning me, demanding to know what had been damaged and whether I had any idea as to who it might be . . . In the canteen I managed to escape to a corner table with Maureen. I must have looked pretty rough, because she kept shooting me concerned glances across the table. Finally she spoke.

'How dreadful for you, Pat.'

'Yeah.'

She silently munched her food for a moment, her eyes on my face.

'I just can't think who'd want to do such a thing,' she said in an aggrieved sort of voice. 'There's no sense in it.'

'Whoever it is . . .' I paused.

'Whoever it is, what?' Maureen asked curiously.

'Whoever it is obviously loathes my guts, don't they?' I said bluntly. 'Either that or they're crazy. Or both.'

'It cuts deeper than that though, surely.' As if adding emphasis to her words, Maureen neatly sliced her egg into two, and the bright yellow yolk trickled onto the plate in a thick pool. 'I mean, take everything that's happened. First of all someone going through your things, then that business with the photographs you told me about . . . Whoever it is obviously resents you.'

'Resents me?'

'What other motive could there be?'

'Why should anyone resent me?'

'Oh, Pat!' A sudden look of irritation crossed Maureen's face. 'How can you ask such a thing? Take a look round. What girl here has your advantages? Your background? A well-off father sending them money every month? And your wardrobe . . . Most of us are lucky if we've more than one coat, let alone the collection you've got.' She shook her head in exasperation. 'And you ask why anyone should resent you!'

I had never heard Maureen speak with such vehemence before, and it momentarily took me aback. She bent her head over her food and continued eating, but I could see a telltale flush of anger slowly spreading over her neck and cheeks.

'Well,' I said rather coldly. 'It's all coming out now, isn't it?'

Maureen looked up at me. 'How d'you mean?'

'The way you feel. After all this time, and now she tells me!'

'I'm not saying *I* resent you, Pat!'

'Like fun you're not!'

Maureen sighed. 'I was simply putting forward the point of view . . .'

'That all the girls resent me. I got the message, it's okay.'

'Oh, Lord.' Maureen pushed her plate to one side. 'You're deliberately taking me the wrong way, Pat. Perhaps some of the girls do resent you, a little bit anyway. But is that extraordinary? Look at it from their point of view. You seem to be one of those . . .'

'One of those what?'

Maureen hesitated. '*Immune* sort of people. Who drift through life with no problems. Yet you seem so discontented half the time. You complain because none of us ever seem to want to go out, all we ever seem to do is sit in our rooms . . . Hasn't it occurred to you that we can't afford to go out? Some of us are actually sending money home, let alone having money sent to us . . .'

'But I offer to help out where I can!' I retorted. 'I often offer to lend you money.'

Maureen studied me carefully, frowning slightly. 'You really don't know what I'm talking about, do you?'

'*You're* saying that the girls resent me because I'm better off than them. And *I'm* saying . . .'

'That's not what I'm saying,' Maureen interjected, 'I'm saying you take everything for granted. You never stop to think what it's like for others. You're okay, so you make the assumption that everyone else is. And that assumption is false, Pat. False and . . .'

'And what?'

She paused, as if weighing up whether or not to speak. Then she said almost reluctantly, 'Thoughtless.'

During the morning I kept thinking about Maureen's words. Try as I did to dismiss them, I felt stung by what she had said. I found myself eyeing all the girls around me, aware for the first time of their hostility. Suddenly it didn't seem to matter any more who had done it, because I felt they were all capable of it. At least in their minds. It was almost as if the burning of my clothes was a kind of general phenomenon, the result of their collective resentment of me . . .

I was sitting about halfway back in the class. Miss Windrup was up in front as usual, drawing a diagram about circulation on the blackboard. She drew these little circles – I think they were supposed to be blood cells or something – and they suddenly reminded me of the scorch marks on my coat. I remembered my coat, forlornly lying in the bottom of the wardrobe, tattooed with dozens of tiny cigarette burns. I must have gasped or something, because I became aware of one or two of the girls eyeing me curiously. All I wanted to do was get out, get away from their cheap curiosity and unspoken hostility. When the coffee-break came I knew what I had to do. Miss Windrup had no sooner dismissed us to the canteen than I was off, sprinting up the corridor towards the nurses' home, taking the stairs two at a time to my room ... And all the time the thought was drumming in my head that the whole thing had been some ghastly mistake. That I was no more suited to nursing than I had been to teaching or any of the other things I'd tried. If I aroused such aggression in one of my colleagues, how could I hope to get the trust and confidence of a patient once I was on the wards?

I didn't feel a flicker of anything as I unlocked the door to my room. You'd think I'd have felt something: apprehension, suspicion, some kind of instinctive awareness of the presence on the other side of the door, but I didn't. I opened that door with no thought in my head except to get out of that hospital as soon as I could. At first all I could see was her silhouette, outlined against the window. She was sitting at the end of my bed, holding a battered old teddy bear that I'd brought from home. She was just sitting there, impassively staring at it when I entered. Then, very slowly, she lifted her vacant blue eyes and stared at me. It was Susan Koppen.

'She seemed such a harmless sort of kid.'

'Yes.' Miss Windrup stirred her tea without looking at me.

'Where is she now?'

'With the doctor still.' Miss Windrup seemed tired, her voice had become oddly strained, and her whole manner was defeated and somehow weary.

It was around lunch-time, and it seemed centuries away from that coffee-break and the discovery of Susan in my room. Miss Windrup had asked me to go into her office but now I was there she seemed preoccupied and distracted.

'How did she get into my room?' I asked.

'Sister Broomstock's making inquiries. But it seems some of the keys in the nurses' home are interchangeable. Hers fitted your lock, it's as simple as that.'

'It's just one of those things, I suppose,' I said, more for the want of something to say than anything else. Miss Windrup glanced at me sharply.

'One of those things?'

'Well . . . She was obviously a bit unbalanced, wasn't she?'

'And if she was, why d'you think she was?'

I shrugged. 'Bad home background. Something like that?'

Miss Windrup gave me a sudden, hard look. 'It's a convenient scapegoat, isn't it? Everything can be blamed onto the background. We're all exonerated from responsibility.'

'You said yourself her home life was dreadful,' I replied, somewhat confused by her attitude. 'That her father drank and her mother . . .'

'Her mother ran off, yes I know.' Miss Windrup stood up and crossed to the window. She stared out for a moment without speaking. Then when she did speak, her voice was flat, and devoid of expression.

'She's what I privately called a slogger. In all the tests, whereas most of you passed with ease, she barely scraped through, sometimes not even that. I once saw her in the library, her head buried in a book. It was the night before your anatomy test . . . I expect the rest of you were all off enjoying yourselves somewhere . . .' Miss Windrup broke off for a second, her eyes fixed on some point out of the window. 'She wanted to see me one evening about a week ago. It was at the end of a class and she came up and asked if she could talk to me. But I was in a hurry.' Miss Windrup's voice was hard. 'I was meeting someone and I didn't want to be late. So I put her off . . .'

The room fell silent. Miss Windrup's back was to me, so I couldn't see her face. I shifted around uneasily in my seat.

'Well,' I said finally. 'It's always easy to be wise after the event.'

'Maybe we shouldn't take the easy way out, then,' Miss Windrup retorted sharply, turning to face me. 'Maybe we should think ahead next time, and then maybe this kind of thing won't happen again.'

'Are you saying . . .' I said slowly, 'that there was something we could have done to avoid it?'

'That's exactly what I'm saying.' Miss Windrup crossed back

to her desk. 'Why d'you think Susan chose your room to attack in the way she did?'

I remembered my breakfast-time conversation with Maureen. 'She was envious, I suppose,' I said. 'She resented me.'

'That's one possibility.' Miss Windrup watched me carefully. 'She might also have been trying to let you know she was there. That she existed. She was a cautious, tentative kind of girl, acutely lacking in confidence. You must have seemed to have things taped to her. To have everything all sewn up. Not just because of your background, but because of your impervious assurance. I think she was trying, in her own way, to puncture that assurance. To make you seem fallible and human, like her . . .'

'Then you're saying it was my fault.'

'Not only yours.' Miss Windrup gave a wry smile. 'I must take my share in it. We all must. All of us who knew her and failed to see the state she was in. How many times did I show her up in class, because she didn't know the answer to some question . . . And you, did it ever occur to you to have lunch with her in the canteen, or sit with her during the coffee-breaks?'

I remembered that lunch when I had abruptly left her to join Jenny Sorrell and the others, and I felt a sudden twinge of guilt.

'That's why I don't want to put it down to "one of those things",' Miss Windrup went on, 'or simply blame her background or mental stability. If we'd all been a bit more thoughtful, perhaps those disadvantages could have been overridden. Who knows?'

My impervious assurance. I went over and over the description that night in bed. It had never really occurred to me that I should strike people in quite that light. I had been too busy looking inward, I suppose. Too aware of my own insecurities, and too busy masking them from the outside world. I suddenly saw myself from Susan Koppen's viewpoint – bumptious, loud, opinionated. I shut my eyes to block out the image, but I couldn't erase it that easily. All at once I felt grateful to that insipid, pallid-faced girl who had felt so violently about me that she had resorted to burning my clothes. I felt grateful because she had deflated me and momentarily thrown me off-course. She had taught me a lesson about myself, and if nothing else was to come out of the whole wretched business, I would at least learn that lesson. I remembered Miss Windrup's words from nearly a week before, when she'd kept me late in the classroom: 'Modify your manner a bit. Learn a bit of humility.'

St. Angela's Hospital

MERICI ROAD
LONDON S.W. 11

HOSPITAL SCHOOL OF NURSING
CONFIDENTIAL REPORT

Surname Morahan **Forenames** Maureen Kathleen

Date of birth 4/2/57 **Expected date of final examination** Autumn 1978

Previous nursing or other relevant qualifications None

Confidential report

Maureen comes from Ballinaslo, a village in South-west Ireland. Her father died some years ago, leaving Maureen's mother to run their small farm singlehanded. Maureen has two younger brothers and a five-year-old sister. She has never visited England before, and this probably accounts for her shyness and hesitancy. Nursing was obviously a childhood ambition with her, and this is apparent in her diligent attitude and sincerity. Maureen has no problems with the practical side of nursing, but seems more uncertain on the academic and theoretical side. Once she has got over her homesickness and has developed more confidence, Maureen should make a good nurse.

Heather Windrup

Heather Windrup, Senior Nursing Tutor

MAUREEN popped briskly through the swing doors of the hospital main corridor into Outpatients. It was another world, a rather seedy, sad world of anxious or bored men and women, old and young, children and babies, littering the benches like castaways. 'It's because they're still the bloody public in there,' Pat was fond of explaining. 'The hospital hasn't really got its hands on them in Outpatients. We haven't stripped them and bathed them, inspected them and labelled them, sterilized them like so many dressings. Out there, patients are still humanity. Ugh!' The last word was softened by a grin but not totally, and Maureen herself had sometimes felt an occasional antipathy towards the great unwashed public. They were much more attractive, cleaner and easier to handle lying in bed, gleaming on the outside if not always on the inside. Like the old woman in the corner, she thought, noting how the woman's dull eyes twitched from the middle distance to the dark, pretty figure of the nurse moving past her and then returned to registering absolutely nothing. But the young man sitting on the opposite end of the same bench missed not a centimetre of Maureen as his eyes travelled from her face to her feet and back again in two swift motions expressing unreserved appreciation. Maureen saw him out of the corner of her left eye. There's impudence for you, she thought. Gosh, those bushy eyebrows, that curly hair – a pound to a penny he was Irish! And she burst out of Outpatients into Pharmacy through more swing doors for all the world like a shooting star. At least, that was how Timothy Ignatius Regan remembered her.

The next time Maureen saw Timothy Ignatius Regan was that afternoon, though she was not aware of it at the time. She and Pat had slipped out to the delicatessen on the corner of Merici Road during their lunch-break to buy some cheesecake. Pat, so she said, was trying to civilize Maureen's palate, alleging that all she probably ever ate at home was mountains of potato washed down with Guinness. Oh, and Irish stew on Sundays and Holy Days of Obligation. Maureen denied this in so far as she insisted she never got the Guinness. The owner of the delicatessen, a bald, sturdy Pole who was forever boasting how he had escaped to England from a German prison camp on roller skates, treated them like royalty, weighing out waist-bulging portions and handing out frankfurters with the indelicate observation, 'I cannot have love with you so I feed you!'

Maureen and Pat were nibbling the frankfurters when Timothy Ignatius Regan appeared at the shop window, dressed like a bus driver – or, more correctly, wearing the uniform hat of a London Transport bus driver and carrying an old and tattered gasmask haversack. He appeared to be examining the window display but his blue eyes were really appraising Maureen again and responding with unconcealed delight. She looked at him or rather through him, because the hat was grubby and too large and it made him look older and nondescript, which was what he wanted. He looked long enough to commit indelibly to memory Maureen's thick dark hair, her broad white forehead, friendly mouth and chin as pert as a robin before he moved off down Merici Road and round the corner out of sight. But not out of mind.

'I got off this morning,' said Maureen as she and Pat were walking back to the hospital. 'Least I'm sure I could have, in Outpatients.'

'What a good idea!' said Pat in the sarcastic manner which came easily to her. 'Why didn't I think of it?'

'Hmm? What are you blathering about?' asked Maureen.

'Well, they can't get away, can they?'

'Who can't?'

'The fractured fibulas in Outpatients. Well, the male fractured fibulas. The presentable male fractured fibulas that is. They're there for the taking. They can hardly run away, can they, with a fractured fibula? Why didn't I think of it?'

'He wasn't a fractured anything,' said Maureen. 'He was an Irish boy and he was very good-looking and I only wish *English* boys were as good-looking!' And she accelerated ahead of Pat and into St Angela's, wiggling her bottom in simulated pique. Timothy duly noted it from across the road where he had appeared wearing a flat tweed cap now, still carrying the tattered haversack and looking exactly like a bookie's runner which, had anybody told him so, would have pleased him immeasurably. Perhaps even more than the sight of Maureen's bottom which made him feel very carnal and determined to meet her. He was pretty sure that it was an Irish bottom, for no reason except that it seemed so very expressive.

The opportunity to meet her occurred at teatime the same day. Timothy thought that he had engineered it, but that was not altogether true. Maureen had gone to the Post Office to send her weekly letter home. There was a postbox in the hospital, but somehow the solid official building that was the Post Office seemed more likely to deal efficiently with her precious letter than the wan little postbox apparently deliberately hidden away in the furthest and darkest corner of the main entrance. She had hardly moved fifty yards from the hospital when she knew that she was being followed. Again it was her extremely good peripheral vision, possibly the result of having been blessed with wide blue eyes, that picked out Timothy walking some yards behind her, still on the opposite pavement, and keeping pace with her. She glanced back for long enough to establish a young man in jeans, blue check shirt, loose short cardigan, and wearing tinted steel-rimmed spectacles. Despite the spectacles there was something vaguely familiar about him and she wrestled with the puzzle for the next fifty yards until the penny suddenly dropped. It was the hair of course, fashionably curly from the crown of the head to the nape of the neck, some curls either brown or black and some a mixture of both. It couldn't be anybody else but the Irish boy from Outpatients, Maureen decided, and glanced quickly across the street again to confirm it.

Her first reaction was to feel irritated. Who did he think he was, following her about the streets like that and after only seeing her the once? Or was he the sort of feller who made a habit of following nurses? She had been one long enough to have discovered that nurses were a natural target for men. 'We're a sex-symbol, darling, like the Bay City Rollers,' Pat used to say. Maureen was tempted to walk across the road and give him a piece of her mind to bring him down a peg, handsome as he was.

At that point she had to cross the street anyway and as she waited on the kerb for a break in the traffic she got her best view to date of Timothy Ignatius Regan: he passed square in front of her, seemingly oblivious of her and then turned into Woolworths which was next door to the Post Office. Maureen's anger began to evaporate. He *was* good-looking, very good-looking, stunning in fact. A lorry sped past her and she had to cling to her cap to stop it being snatched away by the vehicle's slipstream. One hand on her cap, the other clutching her letter, she crossed the road, looking directly as she did so through the store's gigantic window for any sign of Timothy, but there was none.

Was she wrong? she thought, suddenly feeling cheated. Perhaps he was not following her at all! It could have been a coincidence him walking down the same street, even the same street in a place as huge as London. And after all it was a free country – or so the English said, though most of them looked anything but free, scurrying frantically about the place like the little rabbits in *Watership Down*, the book that she was currently reading.

Maureen had mixed feelings as she approached the Post Office and posted her precious letter, not forgetting to allow herself a sentimental second in which to wish that she were going home to Ireland with it. She was staring sightlessly at the list of collection times, which she knew by heart anyway, when an Irish voice behind her said, 'Excuse me, but would you happen to know the cost of a letter to Dublin?'

Maureen grinned at the symbols in front of her. Irish as a peat bog, she said to herself. And immediately felt irritated again. How did he know she was Irish? Why should she know the cost of a letter to Dublin unless he thought she was from there or thereabouts herself? Maureen disliked being instantly labelled Irish, as if she were a piece of linen or a bottle of whiskey. For one thing it distinguished her from the other nurses and also, she suspected, sometimes made her a target for out-of-temper ward sisters and tutors. She hoped only her brogue gave her away now, certainly when wearing her uniform, for she was not yet totally comfortable with jeans and shirts and clogs and the general gaudy ragbag of clothes beloved by English girls. So how had this cheeky feller guessed that she was Irish?

She turned to Timothy and said sharply, 'Sevenpence. For an ordinary letter that is, I wouldn't know about anything else.'

'Well,' he said, 'fancy that. You being from auld Ireland as well!' He grinned broadly.

'Fancy!' she said, almost matching Pat's high standard of

sarcasm. She wanted desperately to ask him how he knew, but why should she bother herself with a perfect stranger, demean herself?

'Sevenpence, you say,' he repeated, still grinning.

'Sevenpence,' said Maureen, her voice still sharp.

'I'll be off and buy the stamp then.'

He took a step towards the Post Office door, paused and said, 'You're not by any chance from Dublin yourself?'

'I am not,' said Maureen.

'You're not.'

'No.'

She was being evasive deliberately, seeing his awkwardness and enjoying it because it was unusual for her to be in control of a conversation with a man. And anyway she thought he deserved to squirm a little.

'Where is it you *are* from?'

'Ballin'slo in Galway.'

'Oh, that place.'

'Know it, do you then?'

'No.'

It was time for Maureen to do her share or the conversation was patently in danger of wilting. She asked, her voice friendly for the first time, 'You're from Dublin yourself then, are you?'

'Wouldn't you know, from the accent?'

'I would not,' said Maureen, which was true because she had not known enough Dubliners to be able to recognize their speech patterns. She thought they tended to talk rather quickly, but then so did everybody who lived beyond the Morahan Farm by the crossroads, where you caught the weekly bus to take you away from a pace of life so slow that speech itself often seemed to be frowned upon, as being altogether too disturbing.

'How long is it you've been over here?' she persisted, wondering suddenly if it was worthwhile because, despite his marvellous looks, the boy seemed exceptionally difficult to talk to.

'Oh, it'll be all of six months now.'

'Long as that?'

'How long have you been over here yourself?'

'Not long. Just the three months.'

'And there you are a nurse already.'

'I wouldn't say that exactly.'

There the conversation expired again and Maureen could not for the life of her think of anything to say to revive it. She looked at his eyes. Were they on the dull side despite their depth of blue and did he squint with the left one ever so slightly? There was a flaw there somewhere but she could not quite identify it. Anyway, he was definitely stupid and it was time that she was getting back to the nurses' home, where Pat had promised to do something exotic to her hair that night.

'Well,' said Maureen, groping for words that would make her retreat positive and quick. They refused to surface so she said lamely, 'I'll have to be going, goodbye now.' She turned, moved to the edge of the pavement, checked that the road was clear and began to cross. She had reached about halfway when she heard him shout, 'The name's Timothy Regan. Timothy Ignatius Regan.' Maureen walked on, reached the opposite pavement, and turned right towards St Angela's. Timothy Ignatius Regan indeed, she thought! There was a mouthful of a name to be sure for somebody who was practically dumb. Still, when he was really stuck for something to say he could always keep repeating his name. Timothy Ignatius Regan indeed! Whoever christened him that? His mother must have been daft, which was probably what *he* was. She resolved to dismiss Timothy Ignatius Regan from her mind. But had she looked back at him, standing where she had left him in front of the Post Office, his tweed cap at a jaunty angle, she would have seen something very disturbing in those deep blue eyes, something menacing: a cold hard determination. And when a portly old gentleman, wishing to examine the collection times, asked politely if Timothy would move aside, he snarled at him viciously, 'Oh, go to hell!'

After tea Maureen went to Pat's room where they shared the cheesecake. It was a bit rich for Maureen's taste, cloying too, but she pretended to like it for her friend's sake. Pat obviously found it delicious, her eyes rolling in ecstasy at every mouthful. 'Isn't this better than spuds?' she taunted Maureen.

'Maybe,' smiled Maureen, 'but not better than spuds and onions. Now there's a meal fit for the Pope!'

Pat made a face. 'What happened to Ireland?' she said. 'It's only what . . . fifty miles from England and yet you're still living in the last century. Well, some of you are.'

'Well, what my dad used to say was that while the English were busy building all these factories and ships and things, the Irish were sitting contemplating on the finer things in life.'

'Like what?'

'Don't be asking me!'

'Didn't your father say what they were?'

'No, he did not.'

'Did you never ask him?'

'I did not. He was that busy contemplating.'

'You're crazy, the lot of you. No wonder so many of you come over here. Like being discharged from a nut house.'

'The English can talk! I've met more nuts over here than ever there are in Ireland. And they're not half so nice with it. Oh, by the way, remember the feller I told you about in Outpatients? Well, he followed me to the Post Office today.'

'And . . . ?'

'His name's Timothy Ignatius Regan.'

'And . . . ?'

'He's a nut,' said Maureen, giggling at her own joke.

'Have some more cheesecake,' said Pat. 'And about your hair, I think it suits you the way it is, don't you? It's not madly fashionable, but it suits you.'

'Does it make me look Irish?'

'Not more so than all the rest of you.'

'Thanks for nothing,' said Maureen, and for some inexplicable reason suddenly hoped that she might see Timothy Ignatius Regan again.

The following day began very badly. She got into a row with Sister Easby for taking clean linen (it was only a pillow case) into the sluice room. Easby gave her the full litany.

'You know what cross-infection is, Nurse?'

'Yes, Sister.'

'What is it?'

'Well, it's exposing a patient to . . . well, to all sorts of other sorts of germs, Sister.'

'So what must we never do?'

'What I've just done with the clean linen, Sister. Take it into the sluice room.'

'Where the risk of cross-infection is high.'

'Yes, Sister.'

'So you do know the rule.'

'Yes, Sister.'

Sister Easby always paused at that point in such a conversation, leaving the atmosphere pregnant with her disapproval. Then she would swiftly deliver the coup-de-grâce, guaranteed to make the most truculent, the most self-confident nurse feel six inches high. On this occasion she said, 'There may be some excuse for ignorance, Nurse, but never for stupidity.'

Not being a truculent or even a particularly confident nurse, Maureen took a stricture rather more to heart than most. It tended to reduce her confidence still further, obliging her to check and re-check even boring old routine procedures like bed-making, pillow-arranging and temperature-taking, so that by the end of the day her body was exhausted and her nerves ragged. As they were at the end of this particular day. When she finally handed over to the night staff, she was so tired and strung-up that she was on the verge of tears and wishing to God she could catch the next boat back to gentle, peaceful Ballinaslo. Pat's suggestion that they should go mad that evening and go see *Gone with the Wind* was more than welcome.

After the film Maureen felt a lot better, principally because she had fallen asleep while the flames were consuming Atlanta and did not wake until Scarlett O'Hara was delivering her final deathless line, 'Tomorrow is another day.' And if it's like today was, God help me, thought Maureen. The cinema was reasonably full and they had to queue to leave. It was when they were shuffling slowly down the staircase to the exit that Timothy Ignatius Regan whispered over Maureen's shoulder, 'Small world, isn't it?' He stayed close behind her until they reached the street.

Maureen was furious. He was definitely following her. She was certain now: this could not possibly be a coincidence. He had followed her and Pat to the cinema and probably sat close to them, staring, snooping, like some unseen camera. She was determined not to speak to him and she took off down the street at such a pace that Pat actually had to run to keep abreast of her. 'Hey, where's the fire?' she asked. 'Do you want to go to the loo, or something?'

'It's him,' hissed Maureen.

'Who?'

'The Irish boy I told you about. He was in the cinema. Followed us there too I shouldn't wonder.'

Pat glanced back.

'Is he dark and wearing a very smart brown suit and horn-rimmed specs?'

'Eh?' The description seemed so unlikely that Maureen, too, glanced back and there sure as fate was Timothy Ignatius Regan, looking like a bank clerk now instead of a bookie's runner, and grinning like a ninny as usual as he followed purposefully in their wake.

'He's not bad-looking, is he?' enthused Pat.

'He's got the cheek of the devil, till you talk to him that is, then he shuts up like a clam. And I'm sick of him keeping following me all over the place. I've a mind to call a policeman.'

'Don't be daft. He looks harmless enough.'

'He's a pest.'

'Well, he's not making *me* run home like a scalded cat.'

Pat slowed her pace to a crawl and despite Maureen's entreaties to 'Get a move on, for Holy Mother's sake,' she maintained that pace until Timothy caught up with her.

'You wouldn't be catching a bus, the pair of you?' he asked breathlessly. 'Miracle how you can walk so fast in those shoes it is.' He indicated Pat's pink platform soles which she did not find particularly comfortable but which she knew formed ideal plinths for her very nice legs.

'You get used to it,' she said, smiling warmly at him and getting a grin like a neon sign in return. Maureen was still walking about a yard ahead, her neck stiff and her shoulders square, plainly trying to convey as much animosity as she could muster.

'I'm Timothy Ignatius Regan,' he announced to Pat.

'So I believe. And I'm Pat.'

'How do you do.'

'How do you do.'

'What . . . what do they call your friend?'

'Ask her.'

'Somehow or other I don't think she'd tell me.'

'Maureen Morahan.'

'Maureen Morahan.' He savoured the name as if it were a line of poetry.

'A countrywoman of yours,' said Pat after a while, feeling it was time to bring him back to earth.

'Yes, from Ballin'slo.'

They were passing a brightly lit pub which plainly gave Timothy an idea. His eyes shone now as he said, 'Would you like to come in and have a drink with me?'

'Me?' queried Pat.

'Well, you and . . . Maureen.'

'Why not?' said Pat. She turned at right angles to enter the pub, calling perfunctorily to Maureen, who was still forging ahead, though not quite so rapidly as at first, 'We're popping in for a drink, Morahan,' and walked into the pub before Maureen could reply.

When Maureen turned round, Pat had vanished and Timothy was standing by the pub door, his smiling face an unspoken invitation which niggled Maureen beyond endurance.

'What's the idea?' she asked, petulant again.

'Your friend was asking if you'd like to have a drink with her . . . and me,' replied Timothy, cute enough to make Pat the actual source of the invitation. 'Just the one,' he added. 'Thirsty work it was following the fortunes of the American Civil War, did you not think so?'

'I'm not thirsty.'

'Well, seems your friend is. She'll be halfway through the first pint by now, perhaps even the second. And it's envying her I am.'

Maureen was trapped. She was full of resentment at having been followed and watched and finally accosted, but she could hardly walk off into the night and leave Pat to endure Timothy Ignatius Regan unaided. At least that was how she rationalized her predicament, though a psychologist might have come up with a rather different explanation for her retracing her steps and walking past Timothy and into the pub with as much of a display of hauteur as a nice girl from Ballinaslo was capable of achieving.

The pub was very crowded. The bar was packed tight as biscuits from one end to the other and the tables were clusters of animated conversation, cigarette smoke and fingers picking energetically away at something greasy in baskets. Maureen stood just inside the door looking round for Pat, whom she eventually traced to the jukebox and a fair-haired young man whom she recognized as a rather raffish medical student. He was not a boy Maureen liked, far too sure of himself for her taste.

Timothy spoke from over her shoulder again. God, it was like having a parrot on her shoulder, thought Maureen in another flash of irritation, provoked as well by the sight of Pat sipping intimately from the medical student's glass.

'Does she know them people then?' he asked.

'She does,' replied Maureen, her lips tight.

'Would you want to be going over there yourself?'

Maureen was now in an even more awkward position than before, if possible. She was reluctant to join Pat and her friend, yet the alternative was to be left alone with Timothy Ignatius Regan. But again subconscious forces intruded and without really being aware of what she was saying, she replied, 'No thanks.' This was all the encouragement that he needed to steer her to a vacant corner of a window seat, sit her down and ask her what she wanted to drink.

'Oh, just a cider,' she said.

'A cider, not something . . . well, stronger?' he asked.

He wouldn't be hoping to get me drunk, thought Maureen, still willing to think the worst of him. But there was no hint of any ulterior motive in his candid, direct stare as he waited for her answer.

'No thanks,' she said, 'a cider would be fine.'

He moved away to the bar and Maureen sat stiffly on the edge of her seat pretending to survey the crowd, but constantly darting quick glances at Pat, who finally recognized her presence with a casual wave. Wait till we get back home, fumed Maureen, she'll get a piece of my mind all right. Coming in here without so much as a by-your-leave and then leaving me stranded with him! She looked towards the bar where Timothy Ignatius Regan had managed to insinuate himself through the crush and was already being served. Good for him, she thought, remembering her own futile and embarrassed efforts to claim attention in crowded pubs in London. What she had not been able to see was just how he had managed it. Timothy Ignatius Regan had simply stuck his elbow firmly into the ribs of an effeminate youth with corn-coloured hair and levered him aside. And when the youth remonstrated, Timothy Ignatius Regan hissed, 'Shut your gob or I'll fill it with me fist.'

Maureen unobtrusively watched him as he returned with the drinks. He did indeed look smart and very respectable in the brown suit with a pale blue shirt and striped tie. Not like the boys at home who tended to look uncomfortable in suits which always seemed too tight across their backs and had sleeves that were too short. Timothy's jacket fitted his slim shoulders perfectly and his shirt cuffs showed a discreet half-inch or so. He looked like a Dublin boy, she decided. Not so different from a London boy really, a thought which somehow pleased her.

'There you are,' he said as he handed her her drink. 'One cider.' He himself had a pint of dark-looking beer, probably Guinness, she guessed. There was a pause. 'Well, good health to you, then,' he said, grinning down at her.

'Good health.'

'Not that I've been having it.'

'Oh?'

'What I was doing at St Angela's. Dislocated my shoulder, I did.'

'How is it?'

'Better.'

They both drank, she sipping her cider which she found too sweet and he drinking in a great gulp which left a tiny rim of froth on his upper lip.

'That was good,' he said. 'Been looking forward to that I had.'

'Yes.'

Another pause developed. Oh no, thought Maureen, it wasn't

going to be like yesterday, with him dumb as a traffic light and her having to keep the conversation going. She looked across at Pat. The medical student was leaning close to her, talking animatedly, and Pat suddenly exploded into laughter loud enough to make people stare, but Pat was oblivious of the attention she was attracting and anyway, Maureen knew that she would not much care. Maureen suddenly felt inadequate and alone. She was very tired again.

The long pause in the conversation which followed was broken when the girl sharing the window seat with Maureen got up and left, leaving room for Timothy to sit down.

'Lucky we are to be both getting a seat,' he said, with as much expression as if he had suddenly found the secret of everlasting life.

'Yes,' said Maureen, sipping her cider again. She was finding it increasingly sickly.

Another pause, but only a brief one this time. 'Did I ask you how long it was you'd been in London?' said Timothy.

'You did.'

'Did I now?'

He was obviously embarrassed and so totally stuck for words Maureen suddenly felt sorry for him.

'Three months,' she said.

'I've been here nearly six.'

'So you told me.'

'Did I now?'

Another pause, mercifully brief. 'I don't like the place, naturally,' he pronounced solemnly. 'Well, who would be liking it?'

'London?'

'England.'

'Oh! Why not?'

'I don't. Not at all.'

'You must have a reason.'

'Oh, I do have, I do that,' he said, with his odd grin, and drank again, which she noticed caused his rather prominent Adam's apple to pulsate. It was then that she remembered.

'I saw you at the delicatessen, didn't I?' she said. It was more an accusation than a question. 'Yesterday. You were wearing a . . . a cap, with a peak, like his.' She indicated an ambulance attendant who was standing nearby.

'What would like him be, then?' He was plainly uneasy.

'He's an ambulance attendant.'

'Me an ambulance attendant! I am not and that's the truth. I'm a brickie's labourer, when I'm in work I am.'

'It *was* you though, wasn't it?' Maureen persisted, working off her earlier irritation. 'Looking through the window of the delicatessen in Merici Road? Yesterday. About dinner-time.' She was certain it had been him. She remembered the cap, but most of all the prominent Adam's apple.

'No, it wasn't me, you're wrong,' he said without much conviction.

'I am not wrong, that I'm not. There's something else as well.'

'And what would that be? It's a right interrogation I'm getting.' He was trying to laugh it off.

'It's your clothes.'

'What about my clothes?'

'You're never dressed in the same things two days together.'

'Well, there's no law against that, now, is there?' He had his back to the wall.

Maureen plunged triumphantly on. 'An old Army jacket or something! You were wearing an old Army jacket when I first spotted you in Outpatients. Yesterday it was jeans and the shirt and the spectacles, like some tourist. And now look at you, like you've just stepped out of a tailor's window. There was the cap, too: there was, Timothy Ignatius Regan. No use denying it. What are you? An actor or something?'

It took him a long time to reply. He had another drink, looked at her as if to speak and then evidently thought better of it. He looked away, rubbed his chin and finally said solemnly, 'It's all part of it.'

'Part of what?'

'Part of what I'm planning on doing here . . . in London.'

'And what would that be, for heaven's sake?'

'Make them pay for their ostentation. The English. For their grand ways and their arrogance and the fact they think we're Hottentots. They do, they think the Irish are Hottentots. Listen to the jokes they make about us. Paddy's a right mug. Paddy's mentally deficient. Well, I'm not mentally deficient even though they do think I'm only fit to dig their holes and hump their building bricks, only when it suits them to let me, that is.'

His voice had risen in pitch and anger until he was almost shouting and several heads turned to look at him.

'Everything's so bloody ostentatious,' he hissed savagely. He must have seen her eyes narrow in disapproval because he immediately apologized. 'Sorry,' he said. 'But it is. Ostentatious. And what right have they, eh? The English, to be ostentatious?' He kept repeating the word as if it explained everything, his behaviour, his anger, even his constantly changing attire.

'It's their own country,' said Maureen lamely. She was more than a little afraid of him.

'Fat lot they ever cared about Ireland being our own country,' said Timothy, his voice lower but still as angry.

That last observation seemed to Maureen to have absolutely no connection with what he had been saying before, so she could see no reason to reply to it, even if she could have thought of something to say.

'Don't you agree with me?' he asked, obviously expecting her to answer.

Oh dear, thought Maureen, becoming bored now. Here we go again. All the old anti-British arguments which crop up every time two or more Irishmen are gathered together. And, she remembered, it didn't even need two sometimes. Old Kevin Flaherty used to sit outside his cottage at home on sunny days, on a stiff-backed dining chair with green upholstery, going over those same arguments with himself for hours on end.

'You do agree with me, don't you, Maureen?'

'It's a Republican you are, then,' she asked him, not really interested.

'Sure I am.'

'You wouldn't be belonging to the . . .?'

She baulked at the word 'Army', for it always sounded sinister to her, especially since the troubles started in Ulster and she read about the death and destruction and bitterness: she could not relate it in any way with her ambition to be a nurse and to help people, as she had once helped Mrs Ryan's cat, putting an elastoplast across its sightless eye which a gander had pecked.

'Not me,' he said boastfully. 'Not Timothy Ignatius Regan. I'm too much my own man to be belonging to any organization. Though I do have the same purpose as they do, that I have.'

'What purpose is that?' asked Maureen, because again it was obviously expected of her.

'To let the ostentatious bastards know I'm here.' He was even quicker to apologize this time. 'Sorry, but some words don't seem to have any nice alternative, do they now?'

'How would you do that?' asked Maureen, thinking how ridiculous he sounded but at the same time feeling uneasy at the coldly fierce way he expressed himself.

'There are ways,' he said, suddenly enigmatic. He took another great gulp of his beer, the prominent Adam's apple pumping strongly when he swallowed. Maureen wondered if that was what gave him his energy.

'They'll soon be knowing about Timothy Ignatius Regan, don't you fret.'

'Why, what are you going to do?' asked Maureen, very uneasy now.

'Ah, that would be telling, wouldn't it?' said Timothy reverting to the handsome Irish boy with the big grin and the stupid eyes. 'If I told you that, there'd be no point me having a peaked cap and tinted specs and all the rest now would there?'

Maureen's natural curiosity took over. 'What *is* the point of having them?'

He grinned but there was no humour in it. He said, 'Well, when I start doing things, I'll need to be disguised, won't I? I mean I don't want them catching me now, do I? I've been practising a bit, haven't I? And all I need before I do start is a bit of money. To buy a few things, you know. I need to be more mobile. Get around this ostentatious bloody country.'

He's mad, thought Maureen. Either that or he was pulling her leg. But was he? She suddenly recognized what the strange thing was about those deep blue eyes. They were not stupid, he did not squint, he just stared when he talked like that, without blinking. Like a cat watching for its prey to appear.

Pat said from out of the chatter and smoke, 'Right, are we going?'

'Going?' Maureen's brain was still obsessed with Timothy. He *was* mad, she decided. He must be. He could not possibly talk like that and be sane.

'Yes, going,' said Pat. 'It's nearly closing time and those people over there want me to go to a club with them, which I really shouldn't, but I shall if I don't get out of here quickly because I rather fancy a club. So are we going home?'

'A club, now there's a grand idea,' said Timothy enthusiastically. 'The night still being young, just like the three of us.'

'No,' said Maureen instantly, 'I'm going home, too.' She got up from the window seat and was halfway to the door before Timothy was on his feet.

'Eh, Maureen, hang on, wait for us,' he called, but she was gone. The door swung shut behind her with finality.

'Mind of her own that girl, has she not?' said Timothy. 'Hadn't we best be going after her and talk some sense into her?' He seemed crestfallen and disappointed.

But Pat advised, 'I wouldn't if I were you.' She sensed that Maureen had already had enough of Timothy Ignatius Regan for one night, as she had had enough of her medical student. And anyway, nursing required that you should not dissipate your energy wantonly. It demanded too much for itself. There was nothing Pat wanted more than to crawl into bed and let sleep look after her for eight hours. And that, she presumed, quite wrongly of course, was what Maureen also wanted.

'I'm sure I can make her change her mind, given half a chance,' persisted Timothy, an edge to his voice.

'She's had a hard day and she's tired. You'll see her again,' Pat added by way of consolation.

'Where would I see her?'

Pat shrugged. 'Are you on the phone?' she asked, trying to be helpful.

'No.'

Pat was stumped and he seemed to be, too. Then he suggested, 'Would you give her my address?'

'Be glad to.'

He found a stub of pencil and scribbled down an address. 'It's by the swimming baths,' he said.

'By the swimming baths. Right, I'll pass that on and then it's up to her, isn't it? 'Night, Timothy.' And Pat, too, left him. He stood looking after her, his face a blank. One of the bar staff, a full-figured redhead, asked amiably, 'Finished with your glass, darling?'

'Piss off,' said Timothy. He walked out of the pub, pushing the door open violently and banging it closed behind him. 'Charming,' observed the full-figured redhead without a trace of animosity. Timothy's behaviour was nothing new to her in the year of Our Lord Nineteen Hundred and Seventy-Five.

Maureen lay in bed staring at the white-painted ceiling which was beginning to flake off round the light fitting, when Pat breezed in to borrow an antiseptic cream for a spot she thought was developing on her chin. Pat had a horror of spots and the slightest blemish on her face was immediately attacked with all sorts of antiseptic creams and lotions.

'It's in the drawer, somewhere,' said Maureen, indicating the desk which though small like the single wardrobe and the single bed still seemed over-large for the tiny oblong room. The furniture looked as if it were just being stored there rather than actually in use and Maureen's sparse personal paraphernalia increased this impression. A girl from Ballinaslo does not acquire much in the way of personal property.

Pat found the cream, squeezed a little onto a paper handkerchief and then sat down at the desk to dab tenderly and suspiciously at the spot, which was more imagined than real. Between dabs she said, 'Will you go and see him?'

'Who?' said Maureen perversely, though she knew very well who Pat was talking about. But she was too tired to be polite, particularly about Timothy Ignatius Regan.

'You know very well who,' said Pat, as she squinted at the mirror.

'Go and see him! That madman? I'd be mad myself if I did, wouldn't I now? It's not me that should be seeing him. It's a doctor.'

'You're exaggerating. I think he's dishy. And let's face it, love.

It's not as if you were up to your eyes in dishy fellers, is it? Thanks for the cream.' And with that Pat moved to go.

'You can be very cruel, Patricia Rutherford,' said Maureen, pouting slightly.

'Not cruel, love, practical,' said Pat. The door closed behind her and Maureen was left pouting at the ceiling. She lay like that for several minutes, running through the events of the day, most of them pretty horrid, she decided. What was she doing here in London anyway? She did not fit into the place, that was certain. Like a nun in a public house she was. Home was where she ought to be; in Ballinaslo, where voices were friendly and there was no constant pressure to remember rules and regulations, pass exams, and wear out your legs to stumps fetching and carrying, lifting, pushing, pulling, watching people die and being too tired sometimes even to care. And all of it without a real friend to share some of the burden with. Pat was all right, but she was an alien, too. She was not Irish: she could not recall her first communion or a coral beach in Connemara or her first Sunday night dance in the school, everybody soap-fresh from Benediction and your heart beating louder than the music when Sean O'Farrell asked you to dance, and before you said 'Yes' you looked automatically at Father Murphy for approval, but he was pouring a nip from his hip flask into a cup of tea. Maybe that's Timothy's trouble, she thought. He felt lonely in spite of the fact that he was from Dublin which was a bit like London, though still not Ireland. She went to sleep with the light still on, and her last thought before she drifted off was that maybe Timothy Ignatius Regan was just all talk and that all he needed was just somebody to tell him to pull himself together and behave. And why should that somebody not be herself? If she did not help him, who would, in London?

The next day a patient died, a little old lady who wore a crocheted cardigan and in a silver locket kept a faded photo of her fiancé killed in the First World War. Miss Hopwood simply faded from a lively-minded, interesting woman to a withered corpse in only a few hours, without pain, without a struggle, almost gratefully. Maureen, who for a fortnight had been Miss Hopwood's 'favourite nurse,' one of several during the old lady's three years at St Angela's, was very upset. She felt even more alone, especially as she stripped Miss Hopwood's empty bed and collected her pathetic worldly goods which were almost as pathetic as her own, thought Maureen. There was the locket, an ebony-backed hairbrush, a prayer book, a pink writing pad and pink envelopes which Miss Hopwood had never used and a tablet of expensive soap, the old lady's only indulgence. Maureen cried a little as she packed them into a large envelope and though Sister Easby saw her, she did not make any comment. She said, 'Hurry up with that bed, please, Nurse,' but in a kindly voice and she did not wait to see that her order was carried out, as she usually did.

Pat was dining out with her parents that night. They were in London on a business-cum-shopping trip. She looked like a model when she came to say goodbye to Maureen. Maureen could see that she was pleased with herself in a long black skirt and with her fur coat draped casually over a green top. After Pat had gone, Maureen sat on her bed and tried to read *Watership Down* but after barely half a page the words became meaningless symbols and she gave up. She reached for her mother's last letter, then decided it would upset her to read it. She sucked a mint toffee and wondered if she should start smoking as most of the other nurses did. It might calm her nerves. Then she thought about Timothy Ignatius Regan again and how he was probably sitting alone just like herself and how ridiculous it was and what harm could it do to go and talk about home even if he was soft in the head. And what was so peculiar about an Irish boy being peculiar? Did her father not invent daily episodes in the life of an imaginary tortoise and had not her grandfather been famous for the rusty old padlock he wore on a string round his neck to ward off consumption? So at half-past eight precisely she made up her mind to call on Timothy Ignatius Regan at the address he had written down.

It took her perhaps ten minutes to walk there, turning into the street at the swimming baths he had described to Pat. It was a mean, exhausted sort of street of terrace houses built some time between the wars. It had steadily declined into its present morose poverty, relieved here and there by a burst of almost surrealist paintwork, undoubtedly the composition of an immigrant family who craved colour. Number thirty-one was typical, gaunt with neglect and with a pair of unrinsed milk bottles on the doorstep. As she knocked, Maureen wondered how there could be a 'B' in Timothy's address, which she had presumed would be either a flat or a bedsitter. The house hardly looked big enough. There was no reply to her first rather timid knock so she knocked again and again with increasing force. She was just about to give up when the door opened and a woman said, 'I was in the back, wasn't I?' It was a reprimand as much as a statement and the woman stood scowling at Maureen, apparently inviting her to argue the point if she dared.

Maureen said, 'Is Timothy Regan at home, please?'

'Who wants to know?' The woman oozed animosity. She looked unprepossessing too, in an old and faded yellow jumper and shapeless dark trousers.

'I'm a friend of his,' said Maureen.

'You're the first one I've ever met,' riposted the woman.

'Is he in?' pressed Maureen, feeling herself becoming angry at the woman's, so far as she was aware, unwarranted unfriendliness.

'No, he's not in and never likely to be again, well, not in this house anyway.'

The clear positiveness of the words coming so suddenly on the heels of the woman's previous prevarication surprised Maureen. But before she could react to them the woman went on, 'So you're a friend of his, are you? Then you can see what I've had to put up with from him, can't you? It's time somebody did.' And she turned abruptly and disappeared into the house which, barely a yard down the hall, was a black void from where Maureen was standing.

'Well, come on in,' the woman's voice ordered from somewhere in the darkness.

Maureen took a tentative couple of steps over the doorstep and down the hall to where a partially open door at the other end of the hall gave a sort of half-light.

'Up here,' the voice ordered again.

Maureen looked up to see the woman halfway up the stairs to her left. They were uncarpeted and Maureen was aware of a slight stickiness as she grasped the bannister and followed the woman.

There was a small landing at the top of the stairs and along it to the right the woman had pushed open what Maureen supposed was a bedroom door. 'In here,' she said.

The first thing Maureen saw when she entered the room was a huge poster of Ché Guevara on the left-hand wall. His bearded face dominated the room, which was not difficult because it was so small, a boxroom in fact. On the right was a camp bed, unmade and littered with newspapers and books, mainly cheap paperbacks and girlie magazines, as was also much of the linoleum-covered floor. The wall above the bed was almost completely obscured by obscene pictures and drawings, while what was left was covered with writing, words written with a ball-point pen, in pencil, in chalk, and even it appeared by the point of a knife or some other sharp intrument. A cheap and stained brown suitcase was partly visible under the bed.

'Well, what do you think of that?' inquired the woman with satisfaction, almost as if she were proud of the mess.

Maureen quickly read some of the larger writing. 'Remember this name – Timothy Ignatius Regan' was crudely printed in letters six inches high across the middle of the wall. 'Death to the English' was similarly scrawled in red biro. She also registered four lines of verse: 'He did not wear his scarlet coat, For blood and wine are red, And blood and wine were on his hands, When they found him with the dead.' Underneath the verse was a huge burst of long lines and dotted lines, tiny figures and parts of tiny figures, presumably representing a violent explosion.

'That's what he did, your friend,' accused the woman, a hint of awe in her voice. 'Wouldn't credit it, would you? Somebody his age! Expect it of a child, but he's a young feller. It was a nice room, but look at it now, ruined.' Her voice trailed off and she picked up one of the books. '*Date with a She-Devil*,' she read from the garish cover. '*Date with a She-Devil*. Would you credit it? What's the world coming to, eh?'

Maureen felt slightly sick, not only because of the compost heap of a room and its atmosphere of evil but because the very air of the house was heavy and stale and there was a smell of grease in her nostrils. She wanted nothing more than to breathe fresh air again and be reassured that all this was quite abnormal, a fetid corner of life light-years removed from Ballinaslo and St Angela's and her own experience.

'I'm sorry,' she said fatuously and bolted from the room, down the stairs and out into the drab street at such a speed that she was panting breathlessly before she had gone ten paces. But she did not slow down and was still running when she reached the swimming baths and turned into the main road. She did slow to a walk then, trying desperately to regain some composure and thanking God for her escape, for that is what it appeared to her to have been. Timothy Ignatius Regan was mad, mad as a cat, sick mad. Thank the Lord he hadn't been there. Holy Mother of God! If he ever followed her again she would definitely call the police. He should be put away, to be sure he should. She was still talking to herself when she reached the nurses' home and the safety of her room where she lay down on her bed, totally exhausted and trembling.

She must have fallen asleep because the next thing she remembered was Pat's voice whispering from somewhere very near, 'Maureen, are you all right, Maureen?' She opened her eyes and there was Pat, flushed and shining from her night out, looking down at her. Maureen felt awful. She was cold, her mouth was dry and her head bursting.

'What are you doing sleeping in your clothes, in your coat?' demanded Pat. 'Did you pass out or something? It's after midnight.'

The last thing Maureen wanted to do was relate her experience to anybody. For one thing it would be difficult to describe the disgust and horror she had felt and secondly she would rather try to blot it from her mind than recall it.

'Just tired,' she said, managing a thin smile. She got off the bed to escape Pat's scrutiny and began to take off her coat.

Pat said, 'You sure you're up to nursing, Morahan? I mean physically? You've looked washed-out for weeks.'

'Who does not?' replied Maureen, even managing to put some tartness into the words because nobody likes being told they look ill even if they do. 'And have you seen yourself some mornings?' she added for good measure.

'Yeah,' said Pat ruefully, 'it's the weather as well, at least that's what I tell myself though I'm a good liar. Do you want anything, aspirin, a sleeping pill?'

'No thanks,' said Maureen, very grateful nevertheless for her friend's concern.

'Right. See you in the morning, then, and don't oversleep because if you oversleep *I* oversleep. Anyway, I thought peasants, like birds, just woke automatically with the dawn.'

'You're a cheeky one, Patricia Rutherford, and no mistake,' said Maureen, trying to be offended and failing miserably.

'Aren't I,' grinned Pat as she moved to the door. 'I'm rich, too, because Daddy gave me twenty-five quid. Oh, and I've got something for you.' She took the folded front and back pages of an evening paper out of her bag, unfolded them and handed them to Maureen. 'There,' she said, indicating the right-hand column of the front page. 'It's incredible.'

Maureen read the headline: 'Bandit dies under bus'. Below it was an account of how Timothy Ignatius Regan, aged twenty and Irish, had walked into a bank in Brixton carrying a haversack which he said contained explosives, and had threatened to blow up the bank and everyone in it if he was not given £10,000. But the counter clerk had called his bluff and raised the alarm; Timothy had fled into the street, to be knocked down and killed by a passing bus. All they found in the haversack was a bus driver's cap, a tweed cap and a pair of tinted spectacles.

'Awful, isn't it?' said Pat. 'He seemed such a nice bloke, a bit wet, but nice.' Maureen was still staring at the newspaper. 'Maureen!' prodded Pat.

Maureen looked up. She handed Pat back her newspaper. She said, 'Goodnight, Pat, and thanks for . . . calling in. I'll be getting to bed properly, now.'

She did get into bed, but for a very long time she was unable to sleep. She lay staring into the darkness, trying hard to think only about home – about Ballinaslo and walking through the cool green lanes there. She pictured young Sean O'Farrell, too; surely he was real, while Timothy Ignatius Regan must have been only an unpleasant dream.

Jean Plaidy
The Georgian Series

The Princess of Celle 70p

True love never ran smoothly for the beautiful Sophia Dorothea, darling of Celle, who first lost her heart to Philip Konigsmarck on her seventh birthday.

At sixteen, a pawn in seventeenth-century German politics, she was forced into marriage with George Lewis, Crown Prince of Hanover and the future George I of England, who cared only for women and war.

Clara von Platen, the uncrowned ruler of Hanover, jealous, ruthless and sexually insatiable, is spurned by Konigsmarck when he re-appears in the life of Sophia Dorothea. In revenge, she plans his ruin – and that of the sad princess he so recklessly loves . . .

Queen in Waiting 80p

The horrors of Saxony and the dilemmas of Hanover faded when Caroline of Ansbach came to England. Her husband, George Augustus, hero of Oudenarde, triumphed as Prince of Wales. Yet the more popular they became, the more George I hated them.

The King was old and sour; his mistresses ugly; his wife, Sophia Dorothea, imprisoned for over twenty years. Pitiless to the Jacobites, he never forgave an insult or an injury.

With her baby dead and her children taken from her care, Caroline determined to take revenge on the man who treated her so cruelly . . .

Caroline the Queen 80p

Never outwardly opposing the will of George II, her conceited choleric husband, Caroline endured constant humiliation for the sake of power. The Queen's tact and intelligence won the admiration of Sir Robert Walpole, the Prime Minister, as between them they strove for peace and prosperity.

The scandals of the Court gave Caroline many problems – astute politicians and personal enemies, a quarrelsome family united only in their dislike for Frederick, Prince of Wales, the concealment of her own ill-health, and a husband who not only boasted to her of his love affairs but asked advice on how best to accomplish some new seduction . . .